One Thing For Sure

David Gifaldi
AR B.L.: 4.2
Points: 6.0

ONE THING
FOR SURE

ONE THING FOR SURE

David Gifaldi

AN AUTHORS GUILD BACKINPRINT.COM EDITION

AN AUTHORS GUILD BACKINPRINT.COM EDITION

Published by iUniverse.com, Inc.

For information address:
iUniverse.com, Inc.
5220 S 16th, Ste. 200
Lincoln, NE 68512
www.iuniverse.com

Originally published by Clarion Books

ISBN: 0-595-15326-7

Printed in the United States of America

For my parents

ONE THING
FOR SURE

ONE

DYLAN MADE HIS nose twitch. Twice. It was becoming a habit. A long time ago he had seen a cartoon wizard twitch just like that. An army of vampire gremlins had chased the wizard to the edge of a cliff. The gray-haired wizard had wiggled his nose and disappeared. Poof!

Dylan's reflection stared back at him from the window of Mr. Aden's beat-up station wagon. He was still visible. The cottage behind him flickered dim and shrunken in the glass. Dylan curled his bare toes into the soft dirt at the edge of the drive and looked down. He always felt stupid afterward. Twelve-year-olds should have more sense, he thought. Magic spells worked only on TV or in Dungeons and Dragons.

Mr. Aden squinted in the sun's glare, his fingers drumming impatiently against his leg. He sighed, then bent down with his cutters. The wire twanged apart; the newspapers seemed to heave a sigh of their own at being released. The stocky man straightened and used the cutters like a pointer to emphasize his words.

"Look, kid, neither of us can afford any more complaints. You've got to be impeccable, perfect. Keep the customers happy. They pay good money to have their papers delivered."

Dylan dropped his gaze from the cutters. He wedged a small, greenish-colored stone between two of his toes, recalling the way Mrs. Bannister's cat had looked up at him with its big green agate eyes. The poor thing was soaking wet from the rain. Dylan had tried the door and found it unlocked. He'd used a kitchen towel to dry off the cat. He hadn't meant to leave the door ajar afterward.

"Sure, you were only trying to help," Mr. Aden added. "But people don't want strangers traipsing through their kitchens. I know you didn't take anything. But some folks think that kind of behavior runs in the family. They don't want to take any chances."

He shrugged.

"Enough said. You're a smart kid. I don't have to spell out everything for you. I've got a list a mile long of kids who'd like this route. Max Dirkwood has been calling my house nearly every night. But up until now you've been the best . . ."

"Max is out to get me!" Dylan yelled, surprised at the hate that shot through his words. He had to look away to regain control. His gaze fell on the tumble-down cabins to his right, their window-eyes shut tight with plywood lids.

Dylan punched the long, thick bangs away from his eyes. What good would it do to tell Mr. Aden about the falling-out he had had with Max? About the Mighty Four? About the way people looked at him now? Better just to keep his mouth shut and pretend everything was all right.

"I should get these delivered," he said finally, gesturing toward the papers.

"I'll second that," Mr. Aden said. "Had a feeling you'd understand what's at stake here."

Dylan watched the old station wagon curve around the half-circle drive and spit up gravel as it swung onto the highway. The Pacific shimmered like a blue mirage behind the roofs of motels and vacation homes in the distance. A sudden breeze started the metal gull spinning atop the rusted sign out front. Dylan dropped to his knees and began rolling and banding the papers. He worked quickly, stopping only once to swipe at his brimming eyes.

When the last paper had been stuffed into the bike basket, Dylan slipped on his sneakers and ran back into the cottage. He poured a half bowl of Cat Chow for Mo, grabbed a T-shirt, and was out again. He'd have to hurry now in order to deliver the papers and still get to the café before the lunch rush.

Charging up to the highway, he was stopped by a wall of cars. The gull on the sign advertising MEL'S COZY COTTAGES creaked above him as he waited for a break in the traffic. Dylan watched the gull spin first one way then the other, its faded wings arched for a flight it would never take. A year ago, when the three of them had first moved into the cottage, the bird had looked so real to Dylan that he had thrown out some bread in an attempt to lure it down. His mother had had a hard time holding back her laughter.

"Stranger things have happened," his father had said to ease Dylan's embarrassment. "Metal or not, maybe that bird *will* fly someday. Maybe it's like a Robertson—just biding its time. When everything's right it will stop its spinning and soar up like an eagle, leaving the rest of the world behind."

Fat chance, Dylan thought, sending a flurry of stones across the road with his shoe. He flinched at the sudden blare of a horn and saw the driver of a passing car wag an angry finger at him. He was tempted to mimic the man by wagging back, but thought better of it. Instead he eyed the twirling gull again. Focusing his concentration, he blinked hard three times. For a moment he actually believed the bird would come alive and soar off, free forever from its metal roost.

*

Dylan swung his right leg over the bar and leapt off, his momentum carrying him a few quick feet. The bike collided riderless against the fence, then crumpled in a heap. Dylan fumbled with his shirt. He knew he was late. He had slowed his pace to make certain no paper skipped into a flower bed or fell short of a doorstep.

Yanking open the back door of the café, he was hit by a tidal wave of heat. The soup pots on the big black stove bubbled steam into the air. The wash area was already stacked high with dirty plates. From the other side of the string-bead curtain came the loud buzz of conversation, along with the clink and clatter of dishes.

Dylan poked his head through the curtain. The place was packed, and the air smelled deep-fried. Mrs. Allioto was busy at the grill. She slapped one burger after the other onto toasted buns, then set the buns into paper-lined baskets brimming with fries. When she noticed Dylan, her eyes swung to the clock.

"I need glasses and silverware right away," the big woman shouted above the din. She pointed to a tub of dirty dishes. "And get these out of here."

Dylan slunk behind the counter. He stuffed a few more plates into the tub and was lugging the works back to the kitchen when he felt a tapping on his shoulder. He turned to see a sunburned girl with a camera dangling from her neck. Short blond curls streamed out from beneath the pink beret that sat at an angle on her head.

"You work here, right?" the girl said.

His arms were straining with the heavy tub. He thought it was a dumb question considering the circumstances, but he nodded anyway.

"Don't suppose you have any bones?"

He shifted nervously. "Bones?"

"A lot of restaurants just throw away their used soup bones. I thought I'd check."

Dylan saw Mrs. Allioto lumbering toward a table in the front with a tray full of lunches. His arms felt as if they would be pulled out of their sockets. "There might be some in the back," he mumbled behind him as he ducked through the curtain.

He heaved the tub onto the sideboard, then began separating the glasses and silver from the huge piles before him. A drop of sweat fell from his forehead and trailed its way down the bridge of his nose as he packed the glasses into racks. He jabbed a finger at the offending drip, then poured a cupful of powdered soap into the plastic funnel on top of the dishwasher. The door slammed with a bang. Water jetted and spurted within as the machine shook into its cycle.

"Hello-o."

Dylan jerked around. The girl rippled her fingers at him. He blew out a sigh and hurried over to the freezer. "Here," he said, holding out a bulging plastic bag. "I guess you could have these. Mrs. Allioto is always complaining about how there's never any room in the freezer. We've got plenty of stock in there already."

"Thanks," the girl said with a smile. Her peeling nose crinkled suddenly, and she rubbed a knuckle over the itch. Then she quickly raised her camera with one hand and clicked a picture.

Dylan's arm reflexed up to cover his face. "Hey, what'd you do that for?"

"Because I'm going to be a photographer, that's why. I need the practice. I'm weak on candid portraits."

"Well, what if I don't want anyone taking my picture?" he replied.

"No harm done. I promise I won't publish it. In fact, if you're so worried about it, I'll destroy the negative. I'll pretend it contains some secret military information, and the President has ordered me to off it."

She puckered her lips and tugged thoughtfully at a curl. "I suppose I could just chop it up into little pieces. But then you never know. Someone might be persistent enough to fetch it out of the trash and glue it all back together. I guess burning or acid would be better. How *do* they do such things? Do you know?"

The dishwasher kicked twice and shuddered to a stop. "You'd better leave," he said. "Mrs. Allioto doesn't seem to be in a very good mood today."

"Sure," she said. "But I think it's terribly insensitive that you don't want to meet my dog Jaws. I only hope I can console him. He likes meeting new people. Not like you."

The girl spun gracefully, and Dylan watched her march back into the restaurant, the bag of bones swinging at her side. A minute later he was behind the counter with the clean silver and glasses. Out of the corner of his eye he saw her sitting with two grown-ups in the back booth. He did a double take. Was she making faces at him? She kept pointing a finger to the side of her face and opening and closing her mouth with exaggerated movements. It was crazy. Like charades. Then he suddenly understood. Jaws!

He hoped he snuffed the smile before it showed. The girl might come over and start talking again. She seemed like the type. The kind who'd ask a zillion questions. Sooner or later the questions would get around to his family. And he'd have to say that he no longer had a father. That his last name just happened to be the same as some stranger now doing time in the Rockport jail.

"A year in the slammer, huh?" Max had yelled across the school hall that awful June day after the hearing.

Yes, he'd have to tell the girl that he was Dylan Robertson—son of a convict.

TWO

DYLAN STEPPED OUT into the blazing afternoon sun. He stuck his hand inside the pocket of his cutoffs, making sure the folded bills that Mrs. Allioto had handed him were safely lodged in the bottom. He had already mentally added the ten dollars to the amount in the mason jar that he kept hidden in his dresser drawer at home. With this week's pay he would have a total of sixty-seven dollars, more than he had ever had at any one time in his life.

He did some quick subtracting. There was still a long way to go, and he couldn't be sure someone wouldn't snatch up the used trail bike at Mr. Bronski's before he had enough. Still, he let his mind drift off, feeling once again the engine humming beneath him, the rush of air slapping against his face as the deep-treaded tires put miles of sandy beach behind him.

The dream ended abruptly. A scrap of paper was woven among the front spokes of his bike. There was writing on it. Dylan untangled the bike from where it had collapsed against the fence, and pulled the note free. He knew at once it was Max's handwriting. His heart picked up speed as he read: *Dragon's Nest at 1500. Level 10. Caution for green. M4.*

It took only a second to decode. He was to be at the driftwood fort at three o'clock. Very important. Use the password. Mighty Four.

The prickling sensation made him shudder. Ever since his father's sentencing, Dylan had stayed clear of Max and the gang. He'd skipped a whole week of school at the end, finding the boys' snide remarks unbearable. Now that school was out, he took long, roundabout routes through town on his way to and from the café— was wary as a tomcat as he delivered his papers. When he did have to pass the arcade or the school yard, he did so quickly, hoping to blur himself like the magazine pictures of cyclists taken at top speed.

Dylan crushed the note and flung it over the fence. He pedaled slowly down the alley and out into the street. There was no need to check the sidewalks and storefronts. The boys would already be at the fort. Waiting. They knew he'd have to come. It would be unthinkable to disregard a Level 10 meeting.

The sand near the water's edge was hard-packed. Dylan rode with the spray from the surf misting his face until he caught sight of the fort in the distance.

The flag that signaled a meeting was a blue dot of color against the white sand and bleached driftwood.

Turning away from the water, he made his way up the beach until the sand became like a bog sucking in his tires. He carried the bike over a graveyard of logs and up onto the wooded bank. Max's new ten-speed shone brightly against the dark, scabby bark of a tree. The two other bikes looked like Model Ts in comparison.

Dylan parked his clunker, then followed the brushed-out path the remaining quarter-mile. He scrambled down the rocky cliffside and stood facing the back of the fort. He could hear their voices filtering through the narrow spaces between the logs.

KEVIN: "What do you do? You've only got four arrows left, and your spear lies shattered at your feet. The beast is barely wounded, and another more hideous creature has sniffed the blood and is on its way toward you."

TRAVIS: "Why not take the boat?"

KEVIN: "You could, but it's filling with water. It got ripped on the rocks, remember?"

MAX: "Is there a bail bucket in the boat?"

KEVIN: "No, but I suppose you could use your quiver."

Dylan broke in. "Seven Sacred Samurai," he said.

"Of the silent tribe of wandering warriors," Max answered immediately. "Enter."

Dylan counted his steps as he walked to the front. There was magic in numbers. He hoped he'd come up with a seven or a nine. They were the most powerful.

". . . eleven, twelve, thirteen." The *worst*. He stood like a statue in the doorway. The three boys were huddled around a ring of colored rocks in the center of the circular space. Max jumped up.

"You've been avoiding us," he accused.

"Yeah, some leader you are," Kevin said, rising to his knees. "For all we know, you could be palling around with Jake or Mickey, giving out all our secrets."

Max nodded smugly. He looked like a teacher listening to his favorite student correctly recite the times tables.

Dylan sucked in a deep breath and looked to Travis. Travis was the most levelheaded of the three. At least he could be. It was Travis who had suggested they use secret ballots for choosing a leader.

Travis raised his chubby fist, thumb uplifted. The fist swiveled suddenly, thumb down.

Max's fiery red hair flopped over his ears as he nodded again.

"I haven't been spreading secrets," Dylan said. "You're crazy if you think that. I've had other things on my mind is all."

"Like what?" Max challenged.

"You know what."

The freckled face became one big smile, and Dylan knew Max would have his day. Max had never gotten over losing the election when the group had first formed and chosen a leader in the spring. "Since my father is a leader in the community," Max had said before the election, "I think it would be only right to choose me as leader of the Mighty Four." Dylan had been shocked when the ballots were counted, and Travis proclaimed *him* the winner. He figured Kevin and Travis had thought Max would be impossible if he won. Things like that went straight to Max's head.

Max slipped a thumb under the waistband of his jeans. "The Mighty Four can't be concerned with anyone's *personal* matters," he said.

The dig hit Dylan like a slab of granite. His hands became fists at his side. "Just say it, coward! Go ahead. Say something about my father!"

Max's eyes turned steel-blue. "Okay, you asked for it," he said. "The fact is you're out. We can't take any chances. Your old man's a criminal. A thief. You've got bad blood. The Mighty Four are now *Three*."

For a moment Dylan went blank. Then he leapt, rushing for Max's legs and throwing him to the ground. The two rolled over, fists flying. Dylan could feel hands tugging at his back, trying to pull him away. He jerked free of the hands.

"Take it back!" he ordered Max. "All of it!"

Max sputtered beneath him. "Thief! Rotten apple!"

Dylan lashed out, but his arms were stopped in midair as Travis collared him. He was thrown back, his head banging against the wall of the fort with a hard, dull thud. The pain spread like lightning.

"That's enough," Travis puffed.

Max was struggling against Kevin's attempts to hold him back. His freckled face had turned scarlet. "Let me at him!" he shrieked.

There was a lull as both fighters caught their breaths. Travis and Kevin relaxed their grips in the false peace. Then, as if both Dylan and Max heard the same soundless bell, they were at each other again . . . sand flinging up around them as their feet and elbows dug for traction.

After a topsy-turvy struggle, Dylan found himself on top. He tried using his knees to pin back Max's shoulders. Max squirmed for release, and Dylan centered his weight to increase his advantage. Then Max's hands groped at his side and catapulted up. The sand B–B'd Dylan's face, filling his eyes. Dylan yelled and stumbled to his feet, backpedaling, blinded. Max lunged. Somehow Dylan found the presence of mind to duck away. Then he planted his feet. His knuckles shot through with pain as Max's jaw gave way to his swing.

This time Travis and Kevin took no chances. Together they pushed Dylan to the doorway. "Go on, get out of here," Travis said.

Dylan could feel the grit in his mouth. His eyes were filling with tears. Through the blur, he saw Max get to his feet and spit out a mouthful of blood. Max spat again, and from his lips dropped a bloody tooth.

"I'll get you for this, Robertson," he said. "Scum. You're a nobody. Just like your old man. I'll get you."

THREE

THE PIPES MADE a terrible clattering sound, shaking the floorboards of the tiny kitchen. Dylan's mother gave the wrench a half turn, putting an end to the racket.

"Mom."

Her welcoming smile went stiff. Fear stamped itself on her face as the dishtowel slid from her fingers.

"My God! What's happened? Dylan!"

She ushered him to a chair and removed his hand from the back of his head. Dylan winced as her fingers probed around the swollen knot there. She moaned, then held his face between her still-damp hands, her gaze darting back and forth, up and down, as she searched for more damage. Dylan watched through burning, slitted eyes. His hand swung up to ease the stinging itch.

"No!" she cried. "You'll only make it worse."

Dylan held the makeshift ice pack to his head. He added pressure slowly as he felt the pain being replaced by a freezing numbness. His mother lowered his neck onto the back of the chair. She propped open an eyelid, then gently squeezed warm water from a soaked washcloth into his eye. His body jolted, and he screamed.

"I know," she said. "But we've got to flush out the sand. There's no other way."

She released the lid, then swabbed the mix of water, tears, and sand from the edge of his eye. Dylan whimpered as she flushed and swabbed the other eye. She toweled him dry and took another look at the bump on his head.

"Do you feel dizzy?"

"No, it just hurts."

She let out a long, low whistle. "No doubt. That's some egg. If it were Easter, we could color it."

He knew she wasn't making fun. It was just her way. Even when she lost her job at the clothes store and had to settle for the maid job at the motel, she had found something to smile about. "At least I'll be getting more exercise," she had said. "A body can get stale standing around behind a counter all day."

Dylan rearranged the cubes of ice and eased the cold washcloth back on the bump. He'd still like to tell that lady down at the store a thing or two. His mother had never said anything about why she was asked to leave. But Dylan knew. Couldn't have a convict's wife selling designer clothes.

His mother sat down facing him. The creases that could only be seen around her eyes when she was worried or sad were now clearly visible. Like tiny dry streambeds.

"Don't you think you should let me in on what happened?"

"I got into a fight."

"I'd say that's pretty obvious. I'll need more than that."

"Max said Dad was a thief. That I had bad blood. They don't want me in the club anymore. They're afraid I might do something. That I can't be trusted."

She closed her eyes. Her body slumped as if someone had dropped something heavy on her shoulders. Then she sat upright again, her eyes springing open and taking on a fierce, determined look.

"Don't you believe it!" she said. "Don't you believe a word of it, Dylan Robertson. Your father . . ." She stopped, her hand suddenly clinching and rising to meet her lips.

Dylan was sorry he had told her. He could have made up some story. Better to lie than to see her get upset this way. The phone rang sharply. Max! He made a move to get it, but she was up, waving him back.

"Hello . . . Yes, this is she . . . Yes, we're just now talking about it . . . No, Dylan doesn't usually get into fights. . . . I see. You probably know we're both going through a hard time right now, Mrs. Dirkwood . . . Yes, I realize that. Perhaps we should hear both sides first . . . I'm sorry that's the way you feel. Mrs. Dirkwood? Hello?"

"What'd she say?" Dylan was out of his chair, his stomach balled-up as if he were back at the fort, scared, but ready to defend himself.

"Max lost a tooth. You didn't tell me. She said you started it."

"No!"

Her voice was calm. "You threw him to the ground."

The pain at the back of his head burst into bloom again. "Yes, but . . ."

She knelt down and grasped his arms, the creases around her eyes deepening. "Don't you see," she said. "There can't be any *buts*. You can't beat up everyone who calls you a name. There are rules, laws, ways a person must act. I won't let you grow up and be like that. I won't. You'll have to cover the cost of Max's dental work. If it's more than you have, I'll pay the rest. I'll find the money somehow. I'm sorry. I know you were saving for the bike. It will have to wait."

Tears welled up in his eyes. He wanted that bike more than anything now. *Had* to have it. That was why he had asked Mrs. Allioto about the dishwashing job for the summer. He was going to show his father that he could get it on his own. His father had a big mouth, always bragging and promising things that never happened.

"I'll get you that bike," his father had promised after they'd rented the bikes from Mr. Bronski and gone riding together that day. "You're a born biker. Got all the right moves. You'll see. That bike will be yours."

Dylan could still kick himself for believing it. Just as he had believed they would hike up to Lost Lake together again. Go fishing. It was always the same. Promises. His father couldn't even stick to a job, let alone a promise. He was like a dragonfly, darting from one pond to the next. Thrumming the air with promises. And hiding secrets under his wings.

The secrets came out at the hearing. His father had been in trouble before. Had broken into a house once. Been caught stealing tools from a construction company he'd worked for. Dylan had been just four-years-old the last time. You can keep secrets from little kids. Even if you told them—said, *Daddy's a thief*—they wouldn't understand.

Dylan thought he was crazy to stick up for his father. Max was right. He did have bad blood. He had his father's blood.

His mother's grasp tightened. "Don't you see?" she repeated. "It was wrong to do that to Max no matter what he said."

He tore himself from her grip. She didn't understand either. No one did. "You're against me too!" he shouted.

Then he was out the door, his feet flying, head down. Frantic to get away. Away from the town, the people, the home that had become like a puzzle whose pieces no longer fit together.

*

He ran till his chest was sore, till the pain at the back of his head no longer mattered. There were no more streets or houses. Just hillocks of sand sprouting purple flowers with pea-pod leaves. Soon the dunes leveled to beach. Before him the ocean crested wave after frothy wave. Dylan walked, shoes and all, into the icy coldness. He stopped when the water reached his knees, his skin suddenly pimpled with goose bumps. Then he turned and made his way slowly through the white-foamed bubbles that crackled in watery whispers around him.

"Hel-lo-o."

The ghostlike sound barely reached his ears through the ocean's roar. Dylan focused his eyes on the two figures rapidly approaching. He could hear barking. The smaller figure took on the shape of an animal, low to the ground, spurting ahead, then backtracking to urge the other on. There was laughter. A girl's laughter.

He was nearly bowled over as the big black Lab charged, its huge front paws sailing through the air and crashing up against his chest.

"Hey, what's the big idea?"

The dog dropped down and lunged at an incoming wave, chomping at the white crest as if it were a bone. The low wave carried the dog back to Dylan. With a happy bark, the dog leapt again, resting its paws on Dylan's shoulders like a dancer.

Dylan felt the dog's warm breath on his face. He wrinkled his nose at the smell and tried stepping out of the animal's grasp. The dog leaned forward and tongued Dylan's ear affectionately. Just then the girl rushed up. It was the same crazy girl who had asked him for the bones and who had made the charade faces at the café. She was gasping for breath and had to hold her stomach as a flood of giggles broke through.

"Down, beast!" she commanded. She pulled the dancing dog from Dylan, then bent to let the dog cover her face with kisses. "You're too fast for me," she said. The Lab barked loudly and shook itself, sending a spray of cold water in all directions. Both Dylan and the girl turned away and cried out at the same time. The dog finished its shakedown, then streaked up the beach as if on the trail of something.

"Hi," the girl said finally. "Small world. I thought it was you."

Dylan tried brushing off the paw prints on his soaked shirt. The prints only smeared. He waited for an apology.

"You couldn't possibly have known it was me from way back there," he said when none came. "You must have been a quarter mile away."

She blinked first one eye, then the other, in rapid succession. "You forget about the photographer's eye," she said. She used both hands to tug down the pink beret that threatened to roll off her thick curls. Her gaze fell to the shallow water lapping her bare feet. Dylan heard the soft cry escape her lips. He watched her plunge a hand into the swirling water.

"Look!" she said. "A sand dollar without even a chip. Here. It's lucky."

Dylan couldn't believe it. He had spent hours during the past year searching for a flawless sand dollar. Now, finally, one had been right there at his feet, and he hadn't even noticed it. He took the shell from her outstretched hand and fingered the delicately etched flower design. His hand folded around the shell's smooth cool surface. It fit perfectly. Even felt lucky. He unlocked his fingers and pushed the shell toward her.

"No, silly," she said. "It's yours. A gift."

He was suddenly embarrassed that he had gotten so miffed at the dog. "Thanks," he said as he slipped the shell into his shirt pocket. "But I don't understand."

"About what?"

"About the photographer's eye. What is it?"

"Oh, that. Well, mine's not fully developed, of course," she replied. "But after you take a lot of pictures, your eyes become trained to notice things. You see things that most people never see—like a plant growing out of a rock, or the way a leaf floats in a mud puddle with its stem pointing up in the air." Her eyes swung up to follow the path of a shrieking gull. "Or how a sea gull lowers its legs like landing gear just before setting down."

He made a face. "Of course sea gulls have to lower their legs before landing. All birds do. Anyone knows that."

"Everyone knows it," she agreed. "But how many people actually watch for it to happen?"

She was right. Although he had seen it happen a thousand times, he had never really *watched* it happen. He tried to picture it now in his mind, but he knew the picture wasn't right. Not exactly. He shrugged.

What difference did it make how a bird lowered its legs, or if a leaf floated stem-up or stem-down in a puddle?

He was glad to see the dog return. It had a thick stick clamped in its mouth, and its tail swished like one of the pennants in front of Mr. Bronski's shop. The big Lab pawed at Dylan's sneakers, throwing its head back in the direction of the water.

Dylan wrenched the stick from the dog's mouth. The dog barked excitedly. Dylan reached back and flung.

"Go get it, boy!" the girl shouted.

The Lab dive-bombed with a splash and plowed its way through the surf. It captured the floating stick, then began its return paddle.

The girl cleared her throat loudly, and Dylan turned to her. She lifted her beret and bowed like someone out of an old-time movie.

"By the way, I'm Amy. I think introductions are in order since it's obvious we'll be running into each other a lot during the next four weeks."

"We will?"

"Well, this *is* a small town, isn't it?"

Too small, Dylan thought. He'd bet there were hundreds of Robertsons in a big city. Even if something did happen in a big city—if your father's picture was in the paper for logging off thousands of dollars worth of trees that didn't belong to him—you could go on and pretend it was someone else's father, someone else's family. Your mother wouldn't have to work as a maid changing dirty sheets because someone was embarrassed to have her talk to their stupid customers.

The dog bounded through the shallows and dropped the stick at Dylan's feet.

"And this intelligent-looking water rat," Amy pointed proudly, "is the one and only Jaws. I'm afraid you've found a friend for life. Once Jaws finds someone to throw for him, he's impossible to get rid of."

The dog's black fur shone like an otter's. Dylan let his hand slide down the sleek wet back. Jaws basked in the attention, then lay on his stomach, facing the stick as if it were about to fly off on its own any second.

After three more throws, Jaws settled down on the sand a few yards away to gnaw on the stick.

"Rest time," Amy announced. "We haven't quite finished the introductions yet, have we? You're Dylan, right?"

"How'd you know?" Dylan said, his voice cracking and finishing high and squeaky. Damn. He hated when that happened.

"You deliver my grandparents' paper . . . Robertson, right?"

He waited for the ax to fall. *I've heard about you,* she would say. *I'm not supposed to get near you. You might run off with my camera, or do something even worse.*

A gust of wind knocked the beret down over her forehead. She took it off and began twirling the pink cap around her finger.

"My grandparents are the Gallaghers. On Lupine Street. They're stuck with me for the next four weeks. My folks left for Europe. Their first vacation alone together in eight years. Sort of a second honeymoon, I guess. It was either stay in Chicago with my brother, who thinks he's the greatest creature ever to walk the earth, or come here to Oregon. My brother lost hands down. Of course, he wasn't exactly broken up over my decision. He says I'm a pain. But he's the real *el jerko* in the house. Do you have any brothers or sisters?"

Dylan shook his head.

"Consider yourself lucky," she said.

She looked out to where the clouds had become lit with a deep orange glow. Dylan breathed easier. She didn't know after all.

"It's beautiful!" Amy gasped. Holding up the camera, she fiddled with the lens and clicked. "Got it. How about one of you and Jaws? Before we go."

She stuck two fingers in her mouth and whistled sharply. Jaws streaked over and sat down in front of Dylan. Amy backpedaled a few steps to take in the ocean and the orange sky.

"Say *whiskey*," she said.

Jaws yelped.

Dylan mouthed the word softly. He felt his lips curve up in a smile. His hand reached for his shirt pocket, feeling the lucky shell within.

FOUR

DYLAN POURED HIMSELF a glass of juice and sat down. Through the half-open bathroom door he could see his mother combing her hair.

"Why don't you make yourself some French toast?" she called. "I slept in longer than I should have."

He watched her apply a thin sheen of pink lipstick. Leaning closer to the mirror, she smacked her lips together lightly. Then she rubbed at the makeup on her eyelids and drew back, smiling.

Dylan took a swig of juice, a flicker of dread rising over him. He knew she would ask him to go with her. She always did. Every Sunday was the same. She'd be happy and full of energy in the morning, looking forward to the drive to Rockport, to her visit at the prison. Only to return later that evening, tired and upset.

He wet his finger and traced a circle around the rim of the glass. His finger wound quicker until the glass began to sing in a high-pitched whine. He had learned the trick from Max two weeks into school last year. They weren't friends then. Dylan was the new kid in class, a role he knew well. Seaview Elementary was his fifth school in three years. He thought he could write a prize-winning essay on what it's like to walk into a strange classroom and have twenty-eight pairs of eyes gawk at you as if you were an alien from some other galaxy.

Dylan had sat alone in the back on that first day of school. He was sorry he hadn't washed the stiffness from his new jeans. Mrs. Carlson called a halt to the chattering and started reading the roll. Finally she came to his name. "Dylan Robertson? Oh, there you are—class, this is Dylan, he's new here. I'm sure you'll all try your best to make him feel welcome."

Welcome? He might just as well have been one of the cutesy kitten posters on the wall. Nobody ever looked at them after the first day. A week passed before Tod Lindholst leaned his bristly head across the aisle and spoke to him for the first time. Dylan had secretly spent several hours studying Tod's shaven head, trying to estimate how long the hairs were. He had decided on a quarter inch, tops. He would have liked to touch Tod's head, just to see what it felt like, and wondered if people with shaven heads caught more colds than people with regular hair. He had concluded that Tod was either a member of that Hare Krishna group, or was practicing for the Marine Corps.

"Yo, Dylan," Tod had said.

Dylan looked over expectantly.

Tod pasted a smile on his face. "I need a couple sheets of paper. How 'bout it?"

Dylan slammed at the release lever of his loose-leaf and handed over the paper. Tod pointed out the smudge marks on one of the sheets. Dylan crumpled up the smudged sheet in disgust, then rifled over another one. Tod nodded, his nose high in the air. Dylan went back to his work, hoping Tod's head would freeze over come winter. He took comfort imagining Tod's head being used as an ice rink by an army of silver-skated head lice.

Of course it hadn't taken long to figure out that Max, Kevin, and Travis were the class big shots. They were the loudest and toughest. The three of them had a strong following because they could be so entertaining. They were always inventing new toys and weapons and things. Dylan had never known you could unscrew the metal top from a pencil until Max unscrewed his and stuck a pin up through the eraser, thereby creating the soon-to-be-outlawed Snub Dart.

"Let's put our inventiveness to use in a less dangerous manner," Mrs. Carlson said after Peggy Blomberg broke the class record for high-jumping from a sitting position—a dart lodged neatly in her left shoulder blade.

It was during the experiment on floating and non-floating objects that Dylan learned how to make a glass sing. Mrs. Carlson was called to the office just as the experiment was starting. Max got his glass beaker really whining. Soon everyone had joined in. The screeching sounded like a pack of crooning coyotes plugged into amplifiers, each animal straining for high C.

Mrs. Carlson stood in the doorway like one of those statues on Easter Island. Everyone waited for her to explode. A couple of girls pointed their fingers at Max. Max raised his hand.

"Mrs. Carlson," he said. "I'm wondering why all the sounds are a different pitch. Does it have something to do with frequency and sound waves? It makes me think."

The woman's face softened immediately. She looked as if she had just been named Teacher of the Year. "This is a perfect example of how scientists work," she said, strutting to her desk. "They often discover things by accident, then ask questions about their accidental findings. All of our knowledge comes from questions like Max's."

As the weeks passed, Dylan still felt like an outcast. He kept touching the air around his desk, making sure there wasn't an electric force field there keeping people out.

Then everything changed. Mrs. Carlson was out for a week in November with the flu. Miss Whitmore took over for her. Max always saved his best tricks for substitutes. The second day Miss Whitmore was there Max slipped a whoopee cushion under Rosemary Isherwood just as she was sitting down. It sounded foul. Miss Whitmore asked for the cushion and told Max he'd have to miss recess. "You're not even a real teacher," Max said. "I only take orders from real teachers." Miss Whitmore was real enough to send him to the office.

Dylan was in the end stall in the boys' room before school the next morning when he heard Max, Kevin, and Travis come stomping in. Max was spitting fire. He was going to get back at Miss Whitmore by rigging the classroom with booby traps. He wanted to take the stoppers off the desk drawer so it would fall out when pulled and make it so every map in the room would fly off its roller when given even the slightest tug. Since Miss Whitmore had scheduled a color-mixing project for art that day, Max planned to loosen all the tops of the paint bottles. "When she lifts the bottles, *whammo!* Her dress will look like a color wheel."

Dylan listened, scarcely breathing. It was just his luck. If the toilet at the cottage hadn't broken down for the umpteenth time, he wouldn't be in this jam.

There was the sound of feet shuffling, then an eerie silence.

"All right, who's in there?" Max suddenly blurted. "Who's the spy?"

Dylan knew he was a goner. There was nothing to do but come out and face the music. He unlocked the door, his gaze falling on Travis first. Travis emptied a half bag of M&M's into his mouth. "You'd better not breathe a word of this," the chubby boy mumbled around the candy.

Max stood with his hands on his hips, smiling. He seemed relieved to see it was Dylan and not someone else. "He won't tell. He hardly says anything anyway. Besides, he knows what would happen if he did."

"Don't worry about me," Dylan said. "I'm no ratter."

Then something clicked inside Dylan. He could almost feel the gears meshing solidly together in his head. The idea floated like a life raft before him. He grabbed hold.

"After yesterday, Miss Whitmore will know it was you if you do all those things," he told Max. He paused until the words stopped ricocheting, then lowered his voice to a whisper. "No one would ever suspect me. I could do it during lunch recess. Miss Whitmore's on duty today. You three can stay close to her on the playground so she'll know you couldn't have done it."

Kevin sniffed haughtily. "You ain't got the guts," he said.

Dylan looked straight at Max. "Try me," he said.

He watched the surprise register on their faces. Then they drew close, and Dylan felt the hands on his shoulders as the huddle was formed. The four of them might have been a football squad planning its next play, deciding on the signals. "Twenty-seven, sixteen, three blue . . . hike!"

Miss Whitmore would get over it, Dylan thought. It was the first time he had ever been quarterback.

*

"DYLAN!" his mother called. "Stop that. You're driving me batty."

His finger halted. The glass stopped its shrieking. Mo the cat padded in, her ears snapping forward from a laid-back position. She eyed Dylan and the glass warily as she headed for her dish.

He finished off the juice in one long swig, then got up and took the eggs from the fridge.

"It's going to be a nice day," his mother said when she came out of the bedroom to check her purse. "We could have a pleasant drive together. Maybe even stop at the zoo, or somewhere for a bite to eat."

Dylan slammed an egg against the side of the bowl and watched the yolk slide to the bottom. He imagined the highwalled prison, the iron gates, the screens through which family members talked with fathers, husbands, sons. It was too scary, too spooky. No, he would never go. He'd promised himself that. There was nothing to say anyway. It wasn't his fault his father had chanced everything and lost. Lost for all of them.

His mother walked over and touched his shoulder. "Why don't you come? Just this once. If you want, you could wait in the truck. You wouldn't have to go in. At least you and I could have some time together for a change."

She wasn't smiling now. There was that sad look deep inside her eyes. He forced himself to pull away from those eyes and went for the bread.

"Dylan?"

He stood with the bread in his hand, listening to the birds chattering outside the open window.

"Okay," she said. "Be good. I'll say hi for you."

He slapped a slice of bread into the bowl and swirled it around, soaking up the yellow goo. A moment later, he heard the pickup roar to a start. He ran to the door. A plume of exhaust rose from behind the truck as it sped down the highway out of sight. The gull swung once around its perch on the sign. "Good morning," it seemed to creak.

"Buzz off," Dylan said.

FIVE

AFTER BREAKFAST, DYLAN got out his receipt book. Although the *Rockport Herald* didn't publish a Sunday paper, he had found that late Sunday mornings were the best for finding people at home.

He saved the Gallaghers for last. It had been three days since he had met Amy and Jaws on the beach. He was beginning to wonder if he would ever see them again. As he pressed the doorbell, a tuneful melody chimed inside. He had to fight the impulse to ring the bell again. People got mad if you rang too many times.

There was a sudden commotion—shouts, footsteps, and a dog's barking. The door opened, and Amy's bright face looked out at him.

"Hi! We were just talking about you."

He froze.

"Don't worry. Nothing bad. Gramps said you usually come to collect about this time every Sunday. He says you're like a clock, and that you deliver the paper in one piece, which is more than the last person did. Come in."

Jaws pranced about the entranceway like a four-legged Boy Scout. He had a red bandanna tied around his neck.

"He likes to get dressed up on Sundays," Amy said.

Dylan smiled and gave the dog a couple of raps on the side. The big dog did his two-footed dance. Dylan scratched him behind the ears and straightened the lopsided bandanna.

Something shifted in the corner of the living room, and Dylan recognized Mr. Gallagher's gray wavy hair and wire-rimmed glasses. The man held a magazine in one hand.

"Right on time," Mr. Gallagher said as he launched himself from the recliner and reached for his wallet.

Mrs. Gallagher peered in from the kitchen. She was holding a potted plant that drooped and a watering can with a long, skinny spout. She looked worried, as if the plant in her hand was suffering from a disease the plant doctor had been unable to diagnose.

"Hi," Dylan said softly when she nodded to him. The woman withdrew from the doorway just as quickly as she had appeared.

Mr. Gallagher shuffled over and handed Dylan the money. "Keep the change," he said, his eyes sparking behind the spectacles. "I've probably said this before, but I know what it's like to deliver papers. I used to have a time of it as a boy trying to keep everyone satisfied. It can be a thankless job sometimes."

Dylan felt the concern behind the words. "Thank you," he said, handing over the receipt.

"You bettcha," Mr. Gallagher replied as he headed back to his magazine.

"I've been working on my photo albums," Amy said. "I can never keep up. I've got pictures from months ago that I haven't mounted yet."

Dylan saw the mass of photos and loose plastic pages spread on the glass coffee table. Other than Amy's work area, the room was in perfect order. There was a polished, clean smell to everything. Dylan thought the rest of the house must be as nice. He was aware that his mouth had gone dry. He made a move to leave, feeling suddenly out of place standing there in the big polished room, but he was stopped by Amy's voice.

"I was getting tired of working on the photos. How's about taking a walk to town for an ice cream? Jaws loves the new bubble-gum flavor at that parlor place."

Dylan looked over to Mr. Gallagher, but the man gave no sign that he had heard.

"Come on, let's," Amy insisted.

"Sure," he said. "Yeah, that'd be fun. I'm all done with my collecting."

Mrs. Gallagher appeared in the doorway again, without the plant this time. "Maybe you should go with the children," she said to her husband. It sounded more like telling then asking.

"Nonsense," Mr. Gallagher said. "We promised to watch over Amy, not shadow her. They'll be okay." He swung around in his chair. "Besides," he said with a grin, "I've got to go sign a peace treaty with those slugs in the garden. I'm prepared to offer them the broccoli if they'll leave the tomatoes and cabbage alone. They drive a hard bargain, the varmints."

Mrs. Gallagher frowned. Her gaze dropped over Dylan. He figured it was the same kind of look she used for inspecting her plants. He half expected her to rush over and look behind his ears in search of aphids or plant rot.

"You just be careful," the woman warned Amy.

"Gram, we're only going five blocks," Amy said as she bounded to the closet and pulled Jaws's leather leash and her camera from a hook there.

Jaws barked when he saw the leash and squeezed himself behind Dylan, pressing his nose against the door, waiting for the first crack of daylight to show through.

"Nevertheless, you be careful, young lady," Mrs. Gallagher repeated.

"I will," Amy said. She looked at Dylan and rolled her eyes.

When they were out of sight of the house, Dylan said, "She didn't want you to go with me."

"Grandmothers are supposed to worry," Amy answered. "They always think you're about six years younger than you really are. She'll be okay."

Dylan nodded. He was glad to be outside again. The sun was a bright fire in the sky, its flames licking his skin and turning the flowers and grass into a fragrant summer stew. He watched Jaws gallop ahead, the dog's red bandanna flowing back like a miniature cape.

"Superdog!" he cried.

They sprinted to catch up.

*

The sidewalks were jammed with loud, happy tourists. Dylan's senses sharpened as Jaws led them into the flow. He made a quick check for signs of Max and the gang. Since most of the locals stayed clear of town on weekends, he thought it unlikely Max would be looking for him here. Still, he couldn't take any chances. Not with Amy along.

"Hey, let's go in," Amy said as they stood in front of an antiques shop. Her attention had been snagged by a display of old camera equipment in the window.

Dylan laughed. "What about him?"

Jaws was leaping up and down, attacking the stuffed hippo that sat in an old high chair in the shop's doorway. The hippo wore a grass skirt and held a sign that said COME ON IN! Jaws had already managed to chew off three or four strands of the skirt.

"Please!" Amy scolded. She tried not to laugh as she marched Jaws to a tiny parklike area near the shop. "If I've told you once, I must have told you a thousand times not to attack grass-skirted stuffed hippos. What will people think?" She knotted the leash around a tree in the park and gave the dog a hug. "Now, you be good. We won't be long. Think bubble gum."

It was cool and musty-smelling inside the shop. The big central room was a maze of old-time furniture. They wound their way to a counter in the back that was covered with weird-looking cameras and movie projectors.

"Wow," Amy said. She picked up an instrument with two glass lenses set in an oval wooden box. It looked something like binoculars, except that it had a handle sticking out from the bottom, and a square, framelike thing about six inches from the eyepiece. Amy put the oval box up to her face. The wood fit like blinders around her eyes. A notched-out area on the bottom slid snugly onto her nose.

"It's a stereoscope," she explained. "Watch."

She took a card from a nearby stack and slipped the card into the frame thing. The card was unlike any Dylan had seen. Half of it was bluish in color, showing a fuzzy image of what looked like a waterfall. But you couldn't be sure. It might just as well have been a tornado whipping across a stormy sky. The other half of the card was just as fuzzy, but red in color. Both images were clearly out of focus.

"You'd better get a card that isn't ruined," Dylan suggested.

"No, silly," Amy said. "Look!"

Dylan took hold of the handle and drew the instrument up to his eyes. It was incredible. The two images had become one and the same. And there was no fuzziness. The waterfall was in perfect focus. You could see the water plunging over the steep rock wall, almost hear it crashing on the boulders below.

"It's Niagara Falls in 3-D," Amy said. "When we went there, we rented raingear and walked through a tunnel onto a platform behind the falls. There was a wire fence so no one would fall or jump off. It was neat. Like taking a shower with your clothes on. Scary too. I kept thinking what would happen if I leaned up against the fence and the wire gave way."

Dylan recalled the drawing he had seen in one of the Believe It or Not books at school. "Is it really true some people used to go over the falls in barrels?"

Amy nodded. "Oh, yeah. They'd have someone secure the top of the barrel after they got in; then the barrel would be tossed into the current. I think they were a little wacko."

"Maybe," Dylan said. But he thought he could understand why someone might try such a stunt. "Well, people would sure think you were brave if you made it. They'd know not to mess with someone who was daring enough to go over the falls in a barrel. Wouldn't matter who you were before."

"But what if you were one of the ones who didn't make it?" Amy said. "If you got smashed or drowned. What then?"

"You're right," Dylan said. "You'd have to make it or it'd just be a dumb thing to do."

A fat man ambled over with a big salesman smile on his face. He wore a string tie with a silver-dollar clasp half covered by the folds of his chin.

"Ah, Niagara Falls! Isn't it lovely? The honeymoon capital of the world. Don't suppose you two are quite old enough for that, though. Not thinking of eloping with your Jedi lunch boxes, are you?"

He boomed a laugh that sent the loose skin on his neck shaking like a rooster's. Then he stopped abruptly and eyed the stereoscope. "An instrument like that would make a fine gift for a parent or friend. And you're certainly in luck today. The stereoscope is on sale."

The man smiled, his yellow teeth spaced out jack-o'-lantern–style. Dylan thought he could see dollar signs flash across the blue-gray eyes.

"I don't think we're looking to buy," Dylan said. He turned the stereoscope over in his hands. "Besides, I don't see any sale sticker."

Amy jabbed an elbow into Dylan's side. "And we've only got a hundred dollars between us," she said with a sigh.

The man's eyes bulged. He bent down. "The sale price is just for you," he whispered, his yellow grin returning. "My boss will probably kill me. But it's the least I can do for two nice kids like you. One hundred dollars, eh?—why, that's exactly what the sale price is. Fancy that. But don't breathe a word of it to anyone, or I'll lose my job for going so low on such a fine piece of equipment."

Dylan thought Amy had gone bonkers. He was about to tell her so when Amy's foot clamped down over his. She stepped forward, hands on hips.

"I can't believe you're trying to sell something that might lead poor innocent children to do a stupid thing like going over Niagara Falls in a barrel. Some people have no conscience."

The man's jaw dropped, his mouth opening to form a big red cave. "I . . ."

"Never mind," Amy continued, her voice rising. "Perhaps if we look around we'll find something more suitable."

She shot a glance at the woman shopper who had drawn closer to listen, then faced the salesman again.

"Have you ever thought how a person's parents would feel if their one and only child plunged to his death? In a barrel? Smashed to *smithereens*? All because of you?"

"What's the problem here?" the woman asked, her face taut with disapproval.

The man held up his hands as if to show he hadn't done anything. He stepped back, blustering.

"Oh, nothing, madam," Amy said. "It just makes me ill to think what this man is proposing. Why, no one in his right mind would try going over such a treacherous falls in a barrel. Come on, Dylan. Let's split this horrible place."

They stood there a second more, like race cars revving their engines. Then they were off, dashing down the aisle, out the door, and careening over to the grass where Jaws lay waiting. Bursting out laughing, they fell to the ground.

"Did you see his face?" Dylan asked. "You were great!"

Amy's heels flailed the ground as another wave of laughter broke over her. "That's the last time he'll try to take advantage of kids," she said.

Dylan giggled on and off the whole way to the Red Raspberry Ice Cream Parlor. After waiting in line to get their cones, he led Amy to an out-of-the-way table on the big wraparound porch. They sat down in the shade of a striped umbrella, and Amy placed Jaws's bubble-gum ice cream down on the paper plate she had asked for. Jaws finished his treat in record time. He licked his chops for more, his tail swishing happily.

"You'll get fat," Amy warned. "That's enough."

Jaws cocked his head to one side, listening and begging at the same time, then settled down on the planks of the porch with a loud sigh.

"Ice cream is his favorite," Amy said. "I felt so sorry for him after the plane ride that I bought him a half gallon just to make up for the awful treatment he had to go through."

"Jaws was with you on the plane?" Dylan asked. He had a picture in his mind of Amy and Jaws sitting side by side, seat belts snugged across their laps, winging their way across the country together. A stewardess appeared in the picture and asked Amy if she wanted some milk. "Yes, please," Amy replied. "A large glass with two straws. My friend is thirsty too."

Dylan smiled.

"They put him in a cage," Amy said. "Then they locked the cage in the baggage compartment with the other animals that were making the trip. I never saw him at all until we landed."

She frowned. "It made me sad to think that he was laid out back there. Do you know they drug the animals? So they won't be nervous in their cages. There I was looking down on mountains and rivers, and poor Jaws was drugged out. Some things aren't fair."

"I've never been on a plane," Dylan confessed. He sat back, using his tongue to press what little ice cream was left into the bottom of his cone. The voices didn't register at first. Then he flinched, his whole body on alert. He peered around the stem of the umbrella, his stomach grinding.

Max, Kevin, and Travis had squealed their bikes to a stop in front of the parlor and were tramping up the porch steps. Their loud chatter was suddenly muffled as they went inside.

"We should go," Dylan said.

"What's your hurry? Hey, you look like you've seen a ghost. Myself, I've never believed in them. But if you know of some great haunted house here in Seaview, I'd be more than willing to explore it with you."

"No. No houses. I mean, let's get out of here. It's too crowded. Please. I'm sure Jaws would rather be someplace with fewer people."

Amy shrugged. "Okay, let's hit the road. Come on, boy."

They threaded their way around the tables to the front. Dylan kept his eyes on the street as he scooted past the window. Only when he had leapt the last two steps and hit the pavement did he look back. He could see the three boys inside. Kevin and Travis were already licking their cones. The girl behind the counter was handing one over to Max.

"Race you to the corner!" Dylan challenged.

Amy streaked off. Dylan's legs pumped hard to keep up.

"What now?" Amy huffed when they reached the curb. "Hey, you're pretty fast."

Dylan leaned forward, hands on knees, to catch his breath. The escape had left a sour taste in his mouth. He thought the thing to do would be to go back and confront Max. So what if he got beat up? At least he wouldn't have to slink around in the shadows anymore, feeling trapped like Jaws must have felt on the plane, like his father must . . .

He shook off the thought and watched as Amy knelt to fix Jaws's bandanna. Though he had only known Amy for a few days, he sure liked her. She made him laugh. If they went back to the parlor, Max and the guys might mouth off about his father. Then Amy would know. She'd ditch him. *No. No sense trying to be brave. Not now.*

"Let's walk back to your place," Dylan said. "I'm kind of tired."

SIX

DYLAN LAY SPRAWLED on the sofa nibbling at a peanut butter sandwich and leafing through an old motorcycle magazine. His mind kept drifting off to Amy and Jaws. He had wanted to say yes to Amy's invitation to stay for dinner. He loved cookouts.

"Gramps usually lets me start the fire," Amy had told him. "You could help. Then maybe we could play some Monopoly, or go down to the beach."

He had stopped himself in the nick of time. He knew how adults could spoil everything with their questions. Like, "Where do you live? What does your father do?"

The sound of the pickup on the gravel outside brought him to attention. He ran to the kitchen to put away the peanut butter and bread. He was smoothing out the old afghan blanket that hid the holes in the sofa's cushions when his mother came in.

She stood for a moment at the door, eyeing the room as if seeing it for the first time. Her dress was wrinkled from sitting, her hair windblown. She looked tired.

"Let's tidy this place up," she said with a sigh. "I want to get some sleep before starting in another week at work tomorrow. I spend so much time cleaning at the motel, I guess I just haven't got the steam to give this place its due. Lucky it's small."

They worked in silence. His mother swept the floors. Dylan sprayed the lemon-smelling cleaner onto a rag and wiped the TV and end tables. Then he held the dustpan for her. He figured the chances were fifty-fifty that she would bring up the visit. He pictured a bag with two marbles in it, one white, the other black. He could see his mother reaching her hand into the bag. He tried steering her fingers toward the white marble.

When they had finished cleaning, his mother cut up some cheese and apple slices and opened a pack of saltines. She motioned for Dylan to join her outside on the two concrete steps that served as a porch. They munched in the rosy evening light. A line of traffic, tourists on their way back to the city, shunted like railway cars on the highway out front.

"Your father's not feeling well," she said suddenly. "He's got a bad cold. He'll be able to see a doctor tomorrow. Other than that he's doing fine."

Dylan watched the apple slice she was holding turn into a black marble. He wondered how fine you could be when you were locked up.

"His spirits are improving. He's been reading a lot. Even started a diary."

Dylan split a cracker into fourths and piled the pieces in a stack on his leg. If she stopped there, he'd change the subject, tell her about Amy and what happened at the antique shop. He knew she'd laugh.

"He misses you and sends his love. It's important for him to know that you feel the same."

Two crows screamed above and landed on the worn patch of grass in front of them. Dylan threw a cracker to each. The birds squawked and raced for the food. Their heads bobbed, and their little black eyes looked up wildly as they ate, as if the offering might be a trap.

"Dylan?"

"I hear you."

"Well?"

He pressed his lips together and traced the veins of his arm with a finger. He imagined being in a hospital room, lying on a bed with tubes and bottles above him. It was the first time he had thought of a blood transfusion. His arm started to ache. It would probably hurt, he thought. Still, people had blood transfusions all the time—flush out the bad stuff and put in the good. He wondered how long it would take.

"Dylan, what are you thinking? Tell me."

"I'm thinking about how much I'd like us to move from here."

"But I thought you liked this town. The ocean. Would you want to leave your friends behind again?"

"What friends?"

She placed a hand on his knee. "You'll make up with Max," she said. "When the bad feelings wear out, you'll make up and things will be like always."

She stared off in the direction of the ocean. "We can't move anywhere else right now," she said. "We're just making it here. When your father gets his parole in a few months, we could talk about moving inland to Conners or Tyler where things are picking up. Then I can stop cleaning up other people's messes and start getting some real skills. I've even thought of driving to Rockport a couple nights a week this fall to attend classes."

Her voice sounded dreamlike. Why couldn't she see? Why couldn't she admit that things were different now? That nothing would ever be the same? He had the urge to grab his mother's shoulders and shake them hard. To make her see. What right had she to wait for his father? Some father he turned out to be. Was she blind? Dylan didn't need a photographer's eye to know how things really were.

*

The next morning he was down on his hands and knees, playing floor hockey with Mo. When she was a kitten, Mo had taken to chasing a tinfoil ball around the house. Dylan could usually get her fired up whenever he wadded up a fresh piece of foil and started throwing it through the legs of the kitchen chairs. He pretended she was a goalie and tried to flick or slap the ball past her. She had developed into quite a pro.

Now, as Mo's eyes stalked his every move, he maneuvered the foil into position and slapped it toward the chair. The cat uncoiled her body, took to the air, and stopped the shot with her right foreleg. She did a flip as she gathered the ball into her paws, then bit down on the foil as though it were a fresh-caught mouse.

He laughed. "Mom, did you see that?"

His mother slid a sandwich into her lunch bag. "Huh?"

"The save; did you see it?"

"Look, I've been thinking," she said. "You're not going to want to hear this, but I think it's about time I phoned Mrs. Dirkwood about Max's tooth."

Dylan groaned. He had thought she might have reconsidered and decided that Max was a creep after all. He was about to protest anew when she shook her hand to shush him. Then she picked up the phone and dialed.

He stomped to his room and threw himself on the bed. It had taken him three months to save the sixty-seven dollars. Most of that was from the paper route. Now that he was helping Mrs. Allioto at the café, the money would pile up even faster. By the end of the summer he would have the hundred and fifty dollars that Mr. Bronski was asking for the bike. *Would have had,* he corrected himself. Now it was hopeless.

"Dylan!"

He rolled off the bed and forced himself back into the kitchen. His mother had her hand clenched on the phone as if she had slammed it down.

"I don't think I like that woman," she said.

He sensed a glimmer of hope in her voice. "Why? What happened?"

"She said she and her husband were more than capable of paying for their son's dental bills, and that the best thing I could do would be to keep my bully son away from her Max. She didn't even thank us for offering."

"You mean I don't have to give up my savings?"

She nodded. "Imagine, the nerve."

Dylan picked up Mo and held her out from him. He spun a circle with the surprised cat staring wide-eyed, its legs pedaling the air for footing.

"Don't," his mother said, lifting a hand to her face to hide a smile. "The poor thing's scared to death."

He let the cat jump to safety, then looked at his mother. The smile was still etched on her face. She wore her brown and orange uniform with the Shepherd's Inn logo embroidered on the pocket. Dylan had always thought it was a dumb name for a motel by the sea.

"Mom," he said. "One thing. I'm no bully. I know that much."

She walked over, ruffled his hair, and placed a quick kiss on his forehead. "I never thought you were," she said. "And you know something? I've got this crazy hunch that the three of us might just make it through all this after all."

Dylan shot a hand through his mussed-up hair. He knew he hadn't heard the last from Max. But at least the bike was still a possibility. And a hunch wasn't something to easily dismiss. Maybe she was right about them making it. The three of them . . . him, his mother, and Mo.

SEVEN

THE CAFÉ WAS CLOSED Mondays, and Dylan hoped Amy would be home when he finished delivering his papers. He could hardly wait to take her down to Mr. Bronski's and show her the bike.

Mr. Aden arrived with the papers and gave Dylan a packet of plastic bags. "Feels like rain," he said in his clipped way. "Better safe than sorry."

Amy was on the front lawn with Jaws when Dylan rode up. Jaws pounded his way over to Dylan and laid a teeth-marked Frisbee at his feet.

"Thank goodness," Amy sighed. "My arm is shot. That dog never gets enough."

Dylan played with Jaws while Amy went in to leave a note for her grandparents. "What's the man's name again?" she yelled from the door.

"Just say the cycle shop," Dylan answered. "There's only one in town. They'll know."

He was surprised when Amy rounded the corner of the house on an old three-speed. The bike was much too big for her. The front tire swerved dangerously as she tried to steer.

"What do you think?" she asked, braking to a stop. Her mouth opened wide when she realized she was going to fall. She slapped a foot to the ground as the bike skidded out from under her.

"I never got much past the training-wheel stage," she said, laughing.

"Never fear," Dylan replied. "Mrs. Carlson taught us first aid last year. I tied the best splints of anyone."

"That's a real comfort to know," Amy said.

Jaws loped beside them as they rode. Dylan went slow so Amy could keep up. Amy's bike squeaked horribly. It must have been in the Gallaghers' garage for eons.

They got off their bikes when they reached Main Street and walked the half block to the squat building that had once been a gas station. Strings of colored pennants rose from the wire fence in front to the roof of the building. The flags flapped noisily in the wind. A large sign above the building's entrance read: MOTORBIKES—DUNE BUGGIES. RENTALS & SALES. A. BRONSKI, PROPRIETOR.

The cycles were lined up in a long row across the face of the building, with a space in the middle separating those for sale from those that Mr. Bronski rented by the day.

"This way," Dylan said.

They passed four shiny new dune buggies, their red metallic bodies glowing like red-hot embers.

Beyond the buggies were several new two-wheelers. Dylan hurried down the row, taking in the wonderful smells of new rubber and vinyl. He didn't stop until he came to the very last bike.

The old Honda was a faded orange in color. There were dents and scrapes on both the front and back fenders. The tires were worn, and one of the side mirrors was cracked. Tiny colonies of rust pocked the silver-gray engine. Dylan stroked the big black rippled seat as if he were petting Mo.

"It doesn't look like much," he said. "But the engine is in super condition. It really purrs. My father said it wouldn't take much at all to get the dents out and repaint it. Dad's a real fixer-upper. You should have seen the go-cart we made once. From nothing but scraps. We're going to work on the bike to . . ."

He stopped, realizing what he had said.

Amy reached for the bike. "Can I sit on it?"

"Sure."

She hopped on, and Dylan showed her where the start button was and how to move the throttle and where the brake was.

"You can ride it all you want once I finally get the money together," he said.

Amy shook her head. "Probably not. I'll be back in boring Chicago by then, fighting with my brother. But thanks anyway. It's neat."

Jaws's ears shot up at the sound of engines firing. Mr. Bronski was shouting instructions to two customers in the rental section of the lot. The young man and woman followed Mr. Bronski's pointing finger and nodded. Then they slowly circled their bikes out into the street. The man stalled his bike and had to start it up again. The woman was laughing. Dylan thought it would be great to go riding with Amy. She'd love it as much as he did.

"Hey, where you been lately?" Mr. Bronski's deep voice boomed across the lot.

Dylan waved. "That's Mr. B.," he told Amy.

"Does he mind us sitting on the bike?"

"Naw, he's all right. I think he's rooting for me, hoping I'll be able to buy the bike before someone else notices it."

Dylan hadn't visited Mr. Bronski in a long time. He told himself it was because he hadn't wanted to run into Max and the gang. Most of the local kids came to Mr. B. when their bikes had flat tires or when a spoke needed replacing. But deep down Dylan was also afraid that Mr. B. might have changed his opinion of him. Maybe Mr. B. didn't want the son of a convict hanging around the place. Maybe Mr. B. thought it ran in the family too.

"Here, it's your turn," Amy said, sliding off the bike.

Dylan jumped on. He twisted the throttle all the way up, pretending he was flying across the sands. He had to stop himself from making engine sounds because he thought Amy might think it was a childish thing to do.

"You look like a real professional," Amy said.

Dylan sat up straight, resting his palms on the sides of the seat. "I don't think I've ever wanted anything as bad as I want this bike," he said.

"Well, then, you'll probably get it," Amy replied. "My mom says if you want something bad enough, you can usually get it. The problem is, most people want too many things. You've got to want just one, she says, not a whole Christmas catalog."

"Cross your fingers for me," Dylan said.

"I'll do better than that." She turned her back to him. "How's this?" she said, swiveling around again to face him. She had her arms, fingers, legs, toes, and eyes crossed.

"Perfect," Dylan laughed. He swung himself off the bike. "If that doesn't work, nothing will. Come on, let's go."

Amy made little grunting noises. "Oh, no," she joked. "I can't untangle myself."

"Zappo!" Dylan said, thrusting out his finger as if breaking a spell.

At once, Amy's body uncoiled. "Thanks," she said. "I was afraid I'd have to go through life as a corkscrew."

"Got a minute to chew the fat?" Mr. Bronski called out from the shop as they passed the doorway.

"Is it okay for Jaws to come in?" Amy asked.

Mr. B. strained his head over the counter, his face suddenly tight with mock fear. "Jaws? Here? In person?"

Dylan smiled. "It's just a dog," he said.

"It's not *just* a dog," Amy corrected him. "It's the incredible wonderdog himself."

The room was cool and dark, and there was a smell of stale cigar smoke in the air. Mr. Bronski stood behind a glass display counter. Inside the case was a variety of small bike parts, as well as souvenir key chains, wallets, and combs with Seaview written on them. The walls of the room were covered with posters and calendars dating back to the 1950s.

Mr. Bronski's gray-streaked hair shot out in tufts from under his fisherman's cap. "I don't suppose Jaws drinks 7-Up," he said as he shuffled to the vending machine.

"No," Amy said., "He's not big on pop. But he loves chocolate."

Mr. Bronski chuckled. "A Lab with a sweet tooth, eh?" He handed Dylan and Amy a can of pop apiece, then lifted the glass countertop and took out a Chunky.

"Here, you'd better feed it to him," he said. "With a name like Jaws, I'm not taking any chances."

"Say thanks," Amy told Jaws as she held out the candy.

Jaws barked, then leapt.

"He should be on TV," Mr. Bronski said. "Anybody who can make something disappear like that should have a show of his own."

There were two stools at the end of the counter, and Dylan and Amy sat down.

"You're a new face," Mr. Bronski said. "A pretty one at that."

Amy turned the color of her beret. Dylan introduced her.

Mr. Bronksi nodded. "Well, welcome to paradise," he said. "At least it was paradise till these clouds began rolling in. It'll be pouring soon, and the tourists will wonder what hit them."

Dylan took a long sip of his pop. He could feel Mr. Bronski's eyes on him.

"How's your mother?"

The soda funneled down the wrong tube. Dylan coughed, his eyes watering. "Okay," he managed to say.

"She's a good woman. Strong. She'll be all right."

Dylan squirmed as if a spotlight had been turned on him. He twirled the can of pop around and around in his hands. When he looked up, he saw Mr. B. gazing out the window to where a party of four were happily strolling through the gate.

"I'd better take care of these folks," he said. "I'll warn them about the clouds, but they won't believe me. Too much sun out there yet. You kids take your time. And stop by again."

"He's sure nice," Amy said when Mr. B. had stepped out the door.

"Yeah. My father did some work for him once. He's never forgotten it. He says it was the best job anyone ever did for him. Dad's good with his hands."

"What does your dad do?" Amy asked.

Dylan felt the muscles in his neck go hard. "He's . . . he's sort of a jack-of-all-trades. You know—some carpentry, mechanics stuff . . . logging."

"That must be handy. My father is all thumbs when it comes to working with tools. He has to call the electrician to change a fuse."

"Aw, that's not true. No one could be that bad."

"Oh, no?" Amy countered. "One time he flooded the basement trying to fix a pipe. It was a lake down there. The city was having a hot spell at the time, and Dad got real miffed when I asked if I could call some friends and have a wading party." She laughed. "Mom said it was the most expensive do-it-yourself job on record. Dad sticks to his teaching and consulting now. He says every person has a place, and that his is at his desk."

Dylan didn't want to think where his father's place was.

Amy talked Dylan into taking her by the school on the way home. "I want to see how it compares to our concrete bunker," she said.

Dylan was in the lead as they passed the school yard. A couple of little kids were climbing the monkey bars, but the rest of the yard was empty. Suddenly there was a shrill whistle. Dylan turned to see Max, Travis, and Kevin playing handball against the gym wall. The three stopped playing and rushed for their bikes. Dylan looked back to Amy, silently pleading with her to hurry.

"I'm a-coming!" Amy said in a fake Southern drawl. "These machines are the con*foundest* things."

The three boys cut Dylan off at the corner, circling their bikes like wolves before a strike. Dylan checked for an escape route. He could cut diagonally across the corner lot and try to outride them. But what about Amy? He slowed to a stop in front of the circling pack. Amy came rambling up a few moments later.

"Well, well," Max snickered as he traced a figure eight with his bike. "Looks like puppy love to me. What's the matter, Dylan? Been bitten by the love bug?"

Kevin started humming the wedding march. "Da dum dee-dum, Da dum dee-dum. First comes love, then comes marriage, then comes Dylan with a baby carriage."

"Who are these creeps?" Amy asked.

Dylan had one eye closed. He snapped his fingers three times in succession. If he had had a wand, he would have waved it.

"Why don't you lugs stop blocking the street," Amy said. She looked to Dylan for support.

Max circled again, gaining speed, then braked to a hard stop right in front of Dylan. The other two boys followed suit. Max opened his mouth and pointed to the gap in his top teeth.

"See this," he said. "I just want you to see it, because you're gonna pay for it. I'm gonna wait till you're not expecting anything. But when Max Dirkwood hits, you'll know it. And your girlfriend too!"

Jaws snarled at the mean-sounding words.

"Whose mutt?" Kevin asked.

Travis started scratching. "I don't know, but the fleabag is dangerous."

"Hard to tell if it's the mutt's fleas or Robertson's," Kevin answered. "The plumbing at the Cozy Shacks must have broken down again."

"His old man probably has the whole prison scratching by now," Max said.

Jaws snarled again. Amy swung her bike toward Dylan. Dylan's gaze fell from her to his handlebars.

"Okay," Max said. "Let's let the baby and his girlie friend through. They're probably going home to play with their paper dolls."

Dylan watched Max and the others pedal back to the school yard, loud snickers trailing behind them. "Let's go," he said to Amy.

"But . . ."

"I said let's *go*!"

He rode hard into the face of the wind. He heard Amy's cry to wait up, but he didn't look back. The rain began as a cooling drizzle, then quickly boiled over into a downpour.

Dylan was soaked by the time he reached Amy's. He skidded to a stop in the shelter of the garage, his legs aching, his stomach churning like a cement mixer. The rain pounded on the roof. Go! he told himself. Leave now while there's still time. Amy must still be blocks away. You'll never have to see her or Max again. You can go home, take the money from the mason jar, hop on a bus, be miles away. Now. Before it's too late.

He swerved the bike around. Jaws appeared at the foot of the driveway with Amy right behind. Dylan clenched the handlebars till his knuckles turned white. He leaned back, his weight sinking into the seat.

Amy's beret was a darker pink from the rain. She parked the three-speed, then slid off her pack and checked the camera inside. "Mr. Bronski should be a weatherman," she said. "Want to go in and dry off?"

Dylan pounded the front tire of his bike against the floor. Water flicked off his bangs and eyelids.

"My father's in jail," he said.

It was the first time he had ever said those words out loud. They sounded foreign to him and made his mouth taste like metal.

"Jail," he repeated. "There's a company that owns a forest, and he and this other guy logged off a whole bunch of their biggest cedar trees and sold them to a mill. They had a secret bank account. Were going to split the money. Around here stealing timber is one of the worst things you can do. Worse even than stealing cars."

He was trembling, his eyes still focused on the concrete floor. "You should know," he murmured. "Because I could—well, because there's no telling when I might . . ."

His mouth was too dry to finish. He tried to swallow, but it was as though something hard had lodged itself between his tonsils.

Out of the corner of his eye, Dylan could see the camera swinging in an arc across Amy's knees. She shifted her weight. "I know about your father," she said. "My grandparents told me. I was wondering if you would mention it. Not that it mattered."

Dylan jerked his head up, unleashing a spray of drops from his hair.

"You know?"

"You said yourself it was a small town."

He watched a miniature river carve a path across the floor. When he looked up again, Amy's face had gone suddenly hard. Her eyes were like ice.

"I'll tell you one thing for sure," she said. "If those lugs back there think they can scare Amy Gallagher, they've got another think coming. That red-haired kid almost made me spit. Your classic bully, that one. But every bully has a weak spot. You can ask Fearless Freddie Maldoon about that."

She nodded slowly, her face easing into a smile.

"Who?" Dylan asked.

"Well, Freddie was a bully, that's all. He was always messing with me, calling me Short Stuff and Iron Mouth because I had to wear braces for a year. He was always picking on the little kids too. He made life especially hard for us girls." She leaned back against the garage wall. "Miss Gillette was our teacher. She was into praising everybody, building up people's confidence and that sort of thing. No matter how trashy you wrote during creative writing, she'd find something nice to say. And she encouraged us to praise one another's work too.

"One day we were reading our stories to the class, and Freddie swaggered up to the front to read his. It was terrible. About some aliens—you know, the green-skinned kind, like out of *E.T.* and every other movie you've ever seen. Even Miss Gillette had a hard time finding some good parts to point out. Then she turned to the class and asked if anyone had anything to say to Freddie for sharing such a nice story.

"That's when I got up and walked to the front. I laid a big, wet sloppy kiss on Freddie's cheek. I'd been fooling around with some chocolate lipstick that my friend Janie had brought to school that day. And when I finished with the kiss, there was a big brown lip mark on Freddie's face. 'Thank you for sharing with us, Freddie,' I said sweetly. His face turned scarlet underneath the lip print. Everyone cracked up because they knew Freddie and I couldn't stand each other.

"Of course, Miss Gillette talked to me after class. She said my response was inappropriate. Then I told her about some of the other things I had thought about doing to Freddie for being such a thug, and she agreed that what I had chosen was a lot better than the rest."

"Really?" Dylan said. "You really did that?"

Amy nodded. "And Freddie's kept his distance ever since. Say, how's about going inside and starting a game of Monopoly."

Dylan curled his toes and felt the water squish inside his shoes. He could hear Amy's voice replaying itself in his head. *One thing for sure . . . One thing for sure. . . .*

64

EIGHT

ONE THING FOR SURE, it didn't take Max long to make good on his threat. Dylan had barely gotten home when the phone rang. It was Mrs. Ramirez. He had to hold the phone away from his ear, she was talking so loud. She had just come home from work to find her paper scattered all over the lawn, soaked. Dylan was speechless. He had wrapped each paper in a plastic bag as Mr. Aden had suggested. There was no way the paper could have blown out of the plastic.

The phone rang again. "What kind of service are you running, boy?" Mr. Ogden's voice cackled through the earpiece. "How am I supposed to read a paper that's waterlogged? My eyes are bad enough as it is!"

Before Dylan had a chance to think about things, two more angry callers had given him *what for*. Mrs. Wickersham said she was phoning the paper and canceling her subscription. "Maybe *The Tribune* has a responsible carrier," she said. "My yard looks like a garbage dump."

Grabbing his jacket, Dylan plowed through the blowing sheets of rain back to town. He took the steps of the new bank building two at a time. The door *shush*ed to a close behind him.

He stood for a moment inside the doorway, his chest heaving from the ride. Two women tellers were laughing in the work area to the right. To the left, behind a waist-high wall, were three desks. A sign on the nearest desk said NEW ACCOUNTS/INFOR-MATION. Dylan stepped from the puddle that was forming at his feet and walked over.

"Yes," the woman said. "May I help you?"

"I want to see Mr. Dirkwood."

"Is this a personal or business call?"

"Personal," he said.

"I'm sorry. Mr. Dirkwood doesn't take personal calls during business hours."

"Well, it's business too," he almost shouted.

"If it's about a new account, I'm the one to talk to." She smiled politely.

"Please," he said. "I have to see him. It's important."

She made a face, her nose wrinkling as if she had caught a whiff of a dead fish thrown up on the beach. She reached for the phone. "Your name?"

"Dylan."

"Dylan?"

"Robertson," he added softly.

"There's a young man to see you, Mr. Dirkwood. A Mr. Dylan Robertson."

The woman got up and strode over to the low wall. A buzzer went off, and a gate popped open. She led Dylan to a door in the back with the words BANK PRESIDENT stenciled in gold lettering on the glass.

Dylan had forgotten how tall Mr. Dirkwood was. The man towered over his desk just as he had towered over the table that one time Max had invited Dylan to stay for supper. "Please have a seat," he said, motioning toward the two leather chairs.

Dylan eyed the chairs. He looked up to the camera monitor that was silently recording the empty chairs from its perch near the ceiling.

"That's okay. I'll stand."

Mr. Dirkwood straightened the knot of his tie and folded his arms on the dark wooden desk. "What can I do for you?" he asked, his clean-shaven face sliding into a smile. Though he had far fewer freckles than Max, the likeness was unmistakable. Dylan imagined a missing tooth on the top right of the man's smile.

"It's about Max."

"Oh, yes. I believe you and Maxwell had a fistfight not long ago." He shook his head. "I've told Max that I don't find such diversions humorous in the least. Fist-fighting and face-bashing might be the order of behavior for some. But not for a Dirkwood."

"I'm not here about the fight," Dylan said. "I'm here about what happened today. About what Max did."

"And what did Max do today?"

Dylan let the words rush out. He told about Max's threats, about the papers, and the angry phone calls.

Mr. Dirkwood had spread the fingers of his hand and was studying his nails. He raised his eyebrows in surprise as if discovering a hangnail. "I see, he said. "And you are absolutely sure it was Maxwell who did this?"

"I *know* it was Max."

The man leaned back in his chair and sighed. He glanced at the photograph of his family that was propped on the side of the desk. Max was there, with his mother and sister, sitting in front of a fake ocean backdrop. All three looked freshly scrubbed and laundered. Max was smiling a shy, innocent smile. His red hair shone under the artificial lighting like a halo around his head.

"It's hard for me to believe that Maxwell would do such a thing," Mr. Dirkwood said. "But you can be sure that I'll talk with him about the matter."

"He'll say he didn't do it," Dylan said. "But he did. He's out to get me because of the fight and because . . ."

Mr. Dirkwood pointed to the papers on his desk. His smile had turned apologetic. "I'm afraid you've caught me at a very busy time. But I promise I will talk to Max. If he admits to this trick, he'll be punished. In the meantime, I guess there's nothing else we can do about it, is there?"

"But I might lose the paper route!"

"I doubt that," came the calm reply. "Accidents happen, and most people are understanding. One mishap like this shouldn't jeopardize your job. But I do appreciate your concern. The best way to do a job is to do it right. That's what I always tell Maxwell."

He rose from the chair and walked around the desk. Dylan was suddenly hit by an airborne wave of after-shave. Mr. Dirkwood placed a hand on his shoulder.

"May I suggest rubber-banding the sacks around the papers in the future. It's amazing what a storm wind can do to things. Why, we had two shutters blown off the house last spring."

Dylan slid from under the hand. He hoped one of the fingers *did* have a hangnail. "Thanks," he said, making his way to the glass door. "Thanks a *lot*!"

Outside, the rain had all but stopped. The street gave off a humid, rubbery smell as Dylan rode to the corner gas station. He looked up Mr. Aden's name in the thin directory and wrote the number with his finger on the steamed-up window of the phone booth. He let the quarter drop and dialed. There was a click at the other end of the line, and Mr. Aden's voice came through.

Dylan breathed in. It was like trying to build up enough courage to jump off the tree at the pond. He knew the longer you waited, the harder it was. He jumped. When he had finished explaining, there was a long silence. Then a grunt.

"Doggone it, Dylan, this is real poor timing. You're sure you bagged every paper?"

"I'm positive."

"Okay. I'll call Mrs. Wickersham and see what I can do. You might have to pay for a week's worth of free papers, though, if that's the only thing that will change her mind. You talk to the others yourself tomorrow. I don't know what else to tell you. Sounds like a personal thing between you and Max. It stinks, I know. But if it happens again, I'll have to let you go. That's just the way it is."

The way it is, Dylan thought after rehooking the phone, *is unfair.*

*

The night air drifted through the screens, carrying the salt smell of low tide.

Dylan studied the map on his lap. He had drawn all the streets and houses of his route. He now placed an X inside the houses where Max had struck. Except for Mrs. Wickersham's, all the X's were on Sutter Drive. It figured. Sutter was a dead-end. All the houses were strung out along the road's east side. Opposite were trees and brush with footpaths that wound down to the beach. It would be easy to melt into the trees and escape to the beach if you were discovered nosing around where you shouldn't be. Dylan was sure the attack on Mrs. Wickersham's paper was an after-thought. Max would have had to take Aspen Street back to town, and he probably couldn't resist the little house that stood so close to the sidewalk.

Dylan hoped he could count on Amy's help for tomorrow's stakeout. If he could catch Max in the act, if he had proof, then maybe Mr. Dirkwood would believe him and do something. Still, it was all so rotten. He had never ratted on anyone in his life. And now Max would be even angrier. There was no telling what he might do, where he would strike next.

The pencil point cracked off under the pressure of his hand. He got up and went to the desk to resharpen it. He found himself eye level with the picture on the wall. *Sure, you go ahead and smile,* he thought.

His father's handsome face beamed out from the picture as if he had heard. The photo was two-years-old now. It had been taken with an instamatic camera the time Dylan and his dad had camped for a weekend at Lost Lake. That was when Dylan had caught his first fish ever. A big rainbow trout. The blue and red speckles were still visible in the picture. The fish hung like a trophy in Dylan's hand. His father had seemed even prouder than Dylan at the time. He had asked another camper to take a picture of the two of them with the fish to show Dylan's mom.

Afterward his father had shown him how to clean the fish. They'd cooked it over the fire with lots of butter and salt. His father had smacked his lips and said it was the best-tasting fish he'd ever eaten. Dylan had wanted the moment to last forever.

Damn!

Dylan reached for the desk drawer. The drawer stuck, and he had to wrench it open. Plunging his hand into the clutter, he found the sharpener, then bent over the basket. The shavings dropped like dead leaves.

"What are you working on?" his mother asked through a yawn.

"Nothing."

"You've ben concentrating so heavily on *nothing*?"

Dylan pointed to the picture. "Why does this have to be here?"

She marked her place and closed the book she'd been reading. "I thought you liked that picture. You were always so proud of it. After all, it was your first fish."

"My first and last," he replied. "Anyway, it's faded. You can hardly make it out anymore. What good is a picture that's all washed out?"

"What do you want me to do with it?"

"I don't know." He reached for the frame, unhooked it, and rehung it with the cardboard backing facing out. "Throw it away. Or store it someplace."

He turned. A hollow feeling came over him. She had that hurt look in her eyes again. His voice softened some. "I just think it's dumb having an ancient picture on the wall."

"Okay, if that's the way you feel."

He slammed the pencil on the desk. "I'm going to bed."

"Good night, then," she answered.

He lay with the light on for a long time, then quickly switched off the lamp when he heard his mother readying for bed. She came out of the bathroom and stopped outside his door.

"You still awake?"

He didn't answer. She probably wanted to talk about the picture. She was always trying to get him to talk lately. As if talking did any good.

"Dylan?"

He kept himself still. If she opened the door, he would shut his eyes and pretend to be asleep. But the door didn't open. Instead, there was the sound of her footsteps. The footsteps grew fainter, then tailed off completely.

"Good," Dylan thought as he snuggled into the mattress. But his eyes wouldn't stay closed. His arms and legs felt suddenly electric, almost aching with the need for movement. He spent the next several minutes thrashing about like someone with a fever, then finally kicked off the sheet altogether. Rolling onto his side again, he noticed the stars twinkling beyond the open window. Eight brights and three dims.

One night last summer Dylan had counted over three hundred stars. His most ever. It had been so hot in the cottage, that he and his father had slept out back in the yard. There was enough of a breeze to keep the bugs away, and they had lain on top of their sleeping bags in just their shorts. Dylan's counting had been stopped by a shooting star that lit up the sky.

"Make a wish!" his father had yelled. "Quick!"

They had been in Seaview for just two weeks, then, and Dylan had wished that things would work out so they could stay. Whoever was in charge of wishes had sure messed up on that one. Things had worked out—but all wrong.

Flopping onto his stomach, Dylan pounded a fresh hollow into his pillow, and tried for sleep once more. But it was no use. Finally he got up and went to the closet where his sleeping bag lay loosely tied with a piece of old clothesline. He took the bag and carried it through the darkness to the window. The bag hit the ground with a soft thud. Dylan climbed onto the sill and jumped through, both feet landing together on the cool grass.

Dragging the bag to the center of the yard, Dylan spread it out and slipped in. The zipper was broken, but the night was more than warm enough. He lay on his back, his arms folded under his head. The stars blinked back at him as he counted.

He fell asleep with the new wish still unspoken on his lips.

NINE

DYLAN WASN'T TAKING any chances the next morning. Although the sky was clear, he bagged each paper securely. He stopped on his rounds to apologize to both Mrs. Ramirez and Mr. Ogden.

"People don't take enough care these days," Mrs. Ramirez told him.

"I wouldn't give half a hoot if my eyes weren't so bad," Mr. Ogden said.

Dylan was relieved to find that Mrs. Wickersham had already left for work. "She was a real hornet over the phone last night," Mr. Aden had said. "She only agreed to stay with us when I offered the free papers."

As he finished the deliveries, Dylan went over his plan to stop Max. There would be no room for mistakes. Mr. Aden wasn't one for beating around the bush. "It's the last time I go to bat for you," he'd said.

Amy burst out the door when Dylan finally rode up to the house. She was wearing a new T-shirt. It was black with fancy white letters. THE PHOTOGRAPH IS MIGHTIER THAN THE SWORD, it said.

"How do you like it?" she asked. "It came in the mail today. Mom had it made special in London. I also got a letter from big brother, but I'm saving it till later."

"It's a nice shirt," Dylan said. "What does it mean?"

"Just what it says. It's like Mom's. The one I always liked. But she's a writer, and hers says THE PEN IS MIGHTIER THAN THE SWORD."

Dylan still wasn't sure what it meant, but he was in a hurry to tell Amy what had happened with the papers.

"He did that?—that fink!"

"Yes, and he might try it again today. I thought maybe you could help me by bringing your camera and staying out of sight. I've got to work at the café, but I'll try to make it back as quick as I can. Then I can take over. If Max or the others should mess with the papers again, we could get a picture as proof."

"Wow," she said. "A real stakeout."

"Let's just hope it works," Dylan answered.

"Can Jaws come? He's always wanted to be a police dog."

Jaws unstuck his nose from the bottom of the hedge and came rushing up, wagging his tail and whining as if begging to be included.

"He doesn't look very vicious."

"That's just part of his disguise," Amy replied. "He pretends to be friendly so as not to give himself away. But underneath that puppy face he's a regular Jack the Ripper."

"I guess it'd be okay," Dylan said. "But you've got to keep him out of sight for it to work."

Amy ran inside for her camera. She had already gotten used to riding the big three-speed and had no trouble keeping up as they rode toward the ocean. When they arrived at Sutter Drive, Dylan pointed out the houses that had been hit the day before.

"I just wish I had a longer lens," Amy said as she set up a lookout post in the brush a few yards from the road. "I've been saving for one, but it's hard to save anything with an allowance of two dollars a week."

She sighed, then focused her camera on the houses. "Well, I think it will still be okay. If he comes, I'll just run out and snap the picture while he's in the act. Then I'll beat it."

"I'll be back as soon as I can," Dylan said. "Good luck. And thanks."

As he hurried to get his work done at the café, Dylan wondered if he should have left Amy all alone. She seemed happy enough to do it, but he thought it was somehow cheating to have a girl help him fight his battles. Still, there was no other way to do it. He couldn't be in both places at once.

By two o'clock he was finished, and he dashed off in the direction of Sutter, checking customer houses on the way. He saw no signs of hanky-panky. The gravel flew up under his tires as he swerved onto the narrow street.

"Amy?"

There was no answer.

Dylan jumped off his bike and ran past the houses. Everything looked okay. He entered the wooded area where he had left Amy at her post and called again.

"Shhhh!" came the low but forceful command.

He made his way over downed trunks and past huge sword-shaped ferns till he saw her. She was lying flat on the ground in a spotlight of sun that filtered through the overhanging leaves, the camera up to her face.

"Everything all right?"

"Shhh, you'll scare it away."

Dylan approached with caution. There was a small pool of dark water between the exposed roots of a large tree. Amy's camera was focused on the pool with its mix of leaves and sticks floating on top. Dylan had to look hard to see the tiny frog. It was riding one of the leaves, as if the leaf was a sailboat. It was colored a much brighter green than the leaf, and Dylan wondered how he could have missed it at first.

Amy clicked a picture. She rose to her knees. "Isn't it neat?" she said. She reached a finger to the leaf and drew in a startled breath as the tiny frog leapt and clasped its webbed feet around her finger. Then she raised her arm so Dylan could see.

The frog's eyes were large and dark, its skin a bright lemony green. The frog jumped off Amy's finger and landed on Dylan's shirt. It hung there and looked up at Dylan, its chest pumping rapidly.

"Better put it back," Amy said. "It looks scared."

Dylan peeled the creature from his shirt and placed it on the edge of the pool. He took a step back, grimacing. He remembered the time he and Max had gone frog hunting together at the pond. There were so many heads, so many eyes poking out of the water. It wasn't something he was proud of—the way they had clubbed at the peering eyes with sticks. At least that was the way he felt now. He wondered why it had seemed so much fun then.

Amy stood up and whistled for Jaws.

"No Max?" Dylan asked.

"Nope. No sign of him or the others either. But I'm glad I came. I got some good shots."

Dylan looked up through the branches of the trees. There wasn't a cloud in the sky. The surf sounded in the distance. "I don't think they're going to show," he said. "They're probably all up at the pond swimming on a day like today."

"Maybe they decided to reform," Amy suggested.

"Not likely. But let's go to the beach. There are some caves I've been meaning to show you, way down on the south end. You can only get to them at low tide."

"Love to," Amy said. "Are there bats?"

"Never seen any."

"Must be tons of them, then," she said, giggling.

"What do you mean?"

"Let's face it, you're not exactly a person who notices things. Look what you're standing in."

Dylan looked down at the clump of pretty green leaves. "Oh no! Why didn't you tell me there was poison oak here?"

"I just noticed it myself. I told you my photographer's eye is still in training. Come on. You can wash off in the ocean."

Dylan eyed the dark pool again, hoping to see the frog one last time before leaving. Amy pointed to the bright green patch on the trunk of the tree. She put her finger to her lips and touched her finger to the frog. The frog jumped off, scurrying under a fern for protection.

"I didn't think so," Amy said. "But you never know."

Dylan gave her a questioning look.

"The prince in the frog's body," she said. "I'm still waiting to find one."

Just then Jaws shot out of a nearby thicket, dragging a three-foot limb behind him. He dropped the stick at Dylan's feet and waited for a throw.

"How am I supposed to throw this monster stick around?" Dylan asked. He caught the twinkling in Amy's eyes. "Never mind," he said, beating her to the punch. "I know . . . *very carefully*."

TEN

THE HEADLAND'S ROCKY wall dropped steeply, butting its foot into the water. A few boulders lay like giant toes at the base, as if testing the temperature of the waves that washed over them.

Dylan led Amy and Jaws over the barnacle-encrusted boulders, then pulled himself up to the narrow shelf that wound round the wall. They followed the shelf until they stood above a thin beach, then picked their way—stepping-stone to stepping-stone—down to the sand.

"It goes on like this for a ways," Dylan said. "Cove after cove."

Amy took in the rock-strewn shore, the clear tide pools, the caves that honeycombed the cliff on the upper end of the beach. She backed out of her thongs, spread her toes in the sand, and was off with a joyful shriek toward one of the caves. Laughing, Dylan kicked his shoes high in the air and followed.

A game of follow-the-leader developed as they darted in and out of the caves, leaping up to touch a rocky ceiling, dropping on all fours to squiggle through a tunnel that led to the next recess. The black walls echoed their whoops. Jaws zigzagged his own course, stopping now and again to check out the scent of a dead crab or to sniff at the tracks of a deer.

Finally they fell exhausted to the sand. The sun sparkled pinpoints of silver over the water. Offshore, the giant rock known as Haystack jutted high into the salted air.

"You can walk all the way out to Haystack when there's a super-low tide," Dylan said.

"You've been there?"

"A couple of times. There's something of a path. Not much, but if you're careful, you can climb to the top. It's like sitting on top of the world." He hesitated. "At least it can be."

Clasping his knees, Dylan rocked backward onto the sand. He let his legs flop down and spread his arms above his head. The last time he had been out to Haystack it hadn't been like sitting on top of the world at all. More like under it.

It was the day they came for his father. A Sunday. Dylan had gone with his dad in the pickup to the new log site. They drove for an hour or more, up and down over dirt roads hemmed in by trees so tall you had to slide down in your seat to see to their tops. Finally they turned off near a creek and bumpety-bumped it up a track barely wide enough to get through.

When they reached the clearing, his father's friend Ernie was already there doing some limbing with one of the chain saws. His truck and trailer had been backed into position a few yards from the felled trees. The truck looked like a serpent with its blunt head and long tail. Dylan waved. Ernie held the screaming saw to one side as he tipped the brim of his soiled cowboy hat in greeting, his cheek ballooned out by a wad of tobacco.

Dylan watched while his father worked the loader, the machine's claw-arm setting the huge cedar logs onto the long trailer. Later he got to ride in the open cab as his father wheeled the loader back into the trees, out of sight. When Ernie left with the logs, Dylan helped his dad load the pickup with smaller stuff. They didn't talk much. His father was always tight-lipped at the sites.

They returned home about suppertime. As they unloaded the truck behind the cottage, Dylan asked again about the bike. His father smiled ear to ear.

"Hell," he said. "You just hold in there a little longer. Ern and I have just about finished the job. You'll have yourself a *new* bike soon, never mind a used one. We're big time now. Been thinking about one of those CT 110s Bronski's got down there. How'd that suit you? Or a big three-wheeler. For the dunes."

The thought of it had made Dylan a little dizzy. His father had said things were looking up since he and Ernie had put in together. But a dune bike was something Dylan had never even considered. The things cost a fortune.

When the two deputies walked around the corner of the cottage, Dylan thought they had come to buy some shakes, or maybe a stack of fence posts. He resisted when his father ordered him inside.

"But supper's almost ready. You wanted to get the truck unloaded."

"Just move," his father had said.

Standing behind the screen door, Dylan could hear the men talking in hushed voices. One of the deputies waved a paper. The other kept clicking away with a camera at the stacks of wood that choked the yard. When Dylan saw the men lead his father around the side of the cottage, he ran yelling for his mother. He followed her to the front door, almost hiding behind her, afraid to look.

"There must be some mistake," his mother had shouted at the men. "Ed, tell them there's been a mistake. Ed!"

But there had been no mistake. Dylan could tell by his father's hard jaw, and by his mother's sudden stiffness when the deputy showed her the paper. While his father was helped into the car, Dylan saw another sheriff's car streak by out front. Lights flashing. Ernie's cowboy hat floating in the back.

"You can follow us if you like, ma'am," one of the deputies said.

His mother's stiffness crumbled then. She tore through the cottage. A moment later the pickup roared to life. And Dylan had stood there as if his shoes were nailed to the ground, his whole body shaking, before pulling himself free and taking off for the beach, his insides on fire.

No, not even Haystack could help that day. Even from the top of the great rock he had felt as though he were standing at the bottom of an elevator shaft, looking up at the slowly descending ceiling. The hum of the motor and the creak of the pulley. The air closing in. . . .

Dylan's hands touched coolness and moisture. His fingers had dug deep below the hot top layer of sand. He swung his head to the side, his neck oiled with sweat. He heard a *ker-plunk,* followed by a howl. Wrenching himself up, he saw Amy jumping up and down in the tide pool, spraying water out at Jaws. She scrambled back to the bank of the pool and leapt out, shaking and dancing the cold from her body. "Come on," she said, shivering in her wet clothes. "The water's warm."

Tearing off his shirt, Dylan sprinted for the pool. He sailed through the air, landing feetfirst. It was like jumping into a tub full of ice cubes. When his feet touched the sandy bottom, he sprang himself up, his head and shoulders shooting out of the ice. "Ye-ow!" he screamed. "Let me out of here!"

They dared each other to jump in one more time.

"We'll get a running start," Amy said, backing away. "On three."

Dylan pedaled back, his body tingling and eager for another shock.

". . . Two . . . Three!"

*

They walked along the water's edge, letting the sun

dry them, and exploring the pools and rocks that were all around. Dylan pointed out a rock whose bottom was covered with orange and purple starfish. One of the smaller starfish was missing an arm.

"I feel sorry for that one," Amy said. "What do you think happened?"

Dylan shrugged. "I've heard they can grow back their arms," he said.

"You're kidding."

"No, they really can. At least that's what people say."

"Too bad people can't do the same," Amy replied. She bent down for a closer look, letting her finger run along the hard spiny back of the four-rayed creature. "Look!" she cried. "It's a lighter color here where the arm was cut off. I think it really is growing back."

When they reached the headland, Amy announced it was snack time. They plopped themselves down in a spot of shade beside the rock wall, and Amy pulled out two apples from her pack. Dylan's stomach growled hungrily. Amy giggled. Dylan felt the blood rush to his face.

"I'm not laughing at you," Amy said. "I'm thinking about the time we had those awful tests last year, the ones every kid in the whole country takes on the same day at the same time. There must have been a hundred of us in the cafeteria. I had been kind of nervous that morning because of the tests and hadn't eaten any breakfast—which was a mistake. My stomach sounded like a caged lion the whole two hours.

"But that was only part of it. Leslie Morganti, Miss Brilliant, kept looking over at me and *tsk*ing her tongue against the roof of her mouth. She even asked one of the teachers if she could move to another seat because my stomach was bothering her. When the results came back, Leslie said it was my fault she scored so low on the vocabulary part of the test. I let her know my stomach apologized, but she just *tsk*ed at me louder than ever. I told her she sounded like a squirrel when she did that. 'You're *detectable*,' she said. When I told her the word was *detestable*, she nearly burst a blood vessel."

Dylan smiled and bit into his apple. The cooling sweetness replaced the dryness of his mouth. He lay down on his stomach and watched Amy rummage through her pack. He expected her to take out her camera, but instead she pulled out a white envelope.

"It's from big brother," she said. "Alias String Bean, alias Mutton Head."

"What does he call you?" Dylan asked.

"I'd rather not be reminded," she said.

Amy read the one-page letter, then took a postcard from the envelope. She broke into laughter. "You won't believe this," she said.

The card was a photo of a dog. The dog wore dark glasses and stood before a microphone, looking like a very new-wave rock-and-roll singer.

"My brother says it reminded him of Jaws."

Dylan took the card. He squirmed forward and placed the card beside the resting Jaws. He laughed.

"There *is* some resemblance," he said. "Too bad we didn't think of something like this. I bet whoever took it had a great time and is making money too."

"*Boing!*" Amy said, her eyelids shooting up like runaway window shades.

"What?"

"That's it. You're a genius. I was down at the drugstore yesterday, picking out some postcards to send back home. There were lots of shots of the beach and the town, but nothing as crazy as this."

Dylan sprang up. "Hey, we could do something even funnier with Jaws. And we could take his picture on the beach, making it something especially for Seaview tourists."

"With a caption like 'Greetings from Seaview,' " Amy put in. "Jaws would be famous!"

"I'm sure Mr. Bronski would take some to sell in his shop," Dylan said. "And Mrs. Allioto too."

"Can you imagine Jaws in dark glasses and a scarf?" Amy blurted.

Dylan could feel the blood banging against his temples. "How about a cigar?" he added. "In honor of Mr. B. And if we made any money, we could split it. You could put your share toward that lens you've been hoping for, and I could put mine toward the bike."

"Why not?" Amy said. "It shouldn't cost that much to get a bunch printed. And people on vacation are always looking for the unusual. Something like this might just catch on."

Dylan was allover goose bumps. "What do you say? Do we jump into this together?"

"Partners," Amy said, offering her hand.

They shook on it. Dylan rose to his feet and stepped out into the sun. He lifted his arms toward the sky like a victorious prize-fighter. He might have thrown a few punches at the air if Amy hadn't been watching. Suddenly he heard something zing past his arm. The pinecone that landed in the sand in front of him was a green oval—its skin new and tough.

"Missed!"

Dylan felt the hair stand up on the back of his neck. He turned. The three boys were perched high atop the headland. Behind them stood a huge mis-shapen evergreen tree, its branches tossed by the wind that whipped across the exposed ridge. The wind lashed at the boys' hair and caught their shirts like sails.

"What gives?" Amy asked.

"Company," Dylan said. "The worst kind."

Amy jumped up and joined him. Jaws followed, racing for the pinecone, his tail flagging with the hope for a game.

Kevin took a step nearer to the edge of the ridge and put his hands up to his face to form a megaphone. "How about a kiss?" he yelled.

"I'll show you mine if you show me yours," came Travis's booming reply.

"Oh, brother," Amy said. "So much for those guys reforming."

Jaws was dancing around with the cone in his mouth. Dylan got the dog to release the cone, then fired it as hard as he could toward the boys. His throw fell far short. "Jerks!" he yelled in frustration. The boys' hands drew back as if on cue. Suddenly the cones were raining down.

"Take cover!" Dylan said. He had barely gotten the words out when his leg was stung by one of the missiles.

They made a dash back to the wall and huddled there, with Amy holding onto Jaws to keep him from running out.

The cones stopped falling. Max's voice was turned to high volume. "The bank is open till five . . . ratter!"

The laughter sounded weak against the rumbling of the waves. But the barrage of squeals that followed came through loud and clear. "*Squeak, squeak, squeak . . .*" Dylan pictured rats in a cage. "*Squeak, squeak, squeak . . .*"

"Will they come down?" Amy asked when the taunting had ended.

"No. They've had their fun."

"How on earth did they find us?"

Dylan rubbed the red spot on his leg. He knew he had let down his guard. "This end of the beach is their territory," he said.

"Are you hurt?"

He shook his head.

"At least we know Max's father talked to him about the papers," Amy said.

"Big help that is."

"It's something. Max knows you're on to him. He'd be taking a big risk to mess with the papers again."

Dylan plowed a deep channel into the sand with one of his heels, then quickly stamped the sides back into the hole.

"Well," Amy said. "We're still partners, aren't we? I mean, with the postcards. It's one heck of an idea."

"Sure," Dylan answered. But he wasn't thinking about any cards just then. Telling on Max had only made matters worse. Dylan felt like a magician who sticks his hand into his hat after saying the wrong words. Instead of a rabbit, he'd pulled out a cobra.

ELEVEN

DYLAN RACED OUT the back door of the cottage to the patch of alder trees. He was looking for just the right size stick. He found a straight one, a little less than a foot long, and gave it a whack against one of the trunks. It sounded good and solid. Then he picked up a handful of leaves from the vine maple and carried both items to the back stoop where Mo was already stretched out in the new-morning sun.

Sitting on the step, Dylan carefully glued several leaves to one half of the stick. He laughed out loud as he set the stick aside to dry. It was perfect. Crazy, but perfect. He pictured Jaws holding the bare end of the stick in his mouth. From a distance, the upper end with the leaves would look like the wrapped tobacco of a cigar.

Amy was steering the big wheelbarrow out of the garage when Dylan rode up.

"Hi, guy! I was afraid you'd overslept."

"No way," Dylan said. He pulled a red silk scarf from one pocket and a pair of old-fashioned earrings from the other. "Mom wishes us luck," he said. "What do you think?"

Amy squealed her approval. She flung the scarf around her neck and lifted the ugly earrings to her ears. "I've always dreamed of being a cover girl," she said, sashaying a few steps down the drive. "You don't think the red clashes with the pink beret, do you?"

"They're brutal together," Dylan said.

"That's what I was afraid of."

Dylan took the cigar-stick from the bike basket and put it up to his mouth. He tapped the end with a finger as if flicking ashes.

Amy laughed. "It's great."

Dylan glanced around the yard. "Speaking of Jaws, where is he?"

"He's in his dressing room," Amy said. "You know how stars are. Actually, he fell asleep while I was brushing him. Lucky I brushed his teeth first."

"You didn't!"

"Wanna bet?" she said. "He's always liked the taste of mint toothpaste. He's the devil on toothbrushes, though."

Dylan smiled. He imagined Jaws on TV. "NINE OUT OF TEN DENTISTS RECOMMEND NEW MINT-O FOR PREVENTING CAVITIES. NEW MINT-O TO GET A DOG'S TEETH THEIR WHITEST. MINT-O FOR SEX APPEAL . . . *Roof, Roof!*"

They flipped over the metal patio table and placed it topside-down on the wheelbarrow. Dylan collapsed the table's umbrella and packed it snugly to one side. Amy loaded a tall drinking glass with a straw, a portable radio, and a box of Doggie Burgers.

"A star is born," Mr. Gallagher said with a chuckle from the back door. "I mean . . . has awakened. Hollywood, I hope you're ready for this."

He pushed open the door, and Jaws streaked out with the Frisbee in his mouth, skidding to a stop in front of Dylan. Dylan pulled the Frisbee from the gleaming teeth and whipped it across the lawn. Jaws tore after it.

"Good idea," Amy said. "We'll take the Frisbee with us and tire him out a little before trying to get him to pose."

The beach was deserted except for a couple of early-morning joggers. Dylan pushed the wheelbarrow over the sand, while Amy held the table steady and made sure none of the other props jiggled out. They stopped a few yards from the water to set up. Dylan flung the Frisbee as hard as he could, and Jaws was off and running.

They skewered the table's legs into the sand until the top was only a foot or so above the ground. It was Dylan's idea to dig a hole for Jaws to sit in. "That way it will really look like he's sitting at the table," he said.

Together they fitted the umbrella pole through the opening in the center of the table and stuck it down into the anchoring sand. Amy released the umbrella's catch and pushed up. The green canopy blossomed overhead. Dylan set out the radio and readied the scarf and earrings while Amy ran to the water to fill the Bugs Bunny glass.

Jaws had forgotten to return with the Frisbee. He was busy nosing around some washed-up seaweed.

"Here, boy!" Amy called. "Over here. Here's a nice cool spot all dug out for you."

Jaws raced over to the hole and began digging at it as though expecting to find a hidden dinosaur bone.

"No," Amy said. "Just sit."

Dylan laughed and tossed Amy a packet of Doggie Burgers. Amy used one of the patties to position Jaws in the hole. "There you go," she said. "Good."

"Hmmm, good," Dylan giggled as he wrapped the scarf around Jaws's neck and knotted it loosely. Jaws finished his snack and twisted his head from side to side in an attempt to get at the scarf's ends, which danced airily in the breeze.

Dylan drew the dog's attention away from the scarf with another burger. "You'd better get the camera ready," he said. "I don't think we're going to have a lot of time."

Jaws tried leaping out of the hole when Amy ran to the front.

"No!" Dylan cried, pulling him back. He picked up the cigar-stick, and Jaws eagerly clamped down on it. Quickly Dylan attached an earring to Jaws's left ear. Jaws swung around, hitting the table. The glass of water spilled, and the radio toppled on its side. Dylan screamed as the icy water washed over his bare leg.

"Amy! Help!"

"Just forget the other earring," Amy said. She was down on her knees, the camera up to her face, her hand turning madly as she focused. "The cigar!" she yelled. "He dropped it. Put it back."

Dylan picked up the stick. Jaws barked. "Here you go, boy. Here it is."

"Oh, no," Amy said. "We forgot the beret." She tore the beret from her head and flung it. Dylan caught the cap. He quickly reset the glass and righted the radio. Then he laid the cap on Jaws's head.

"Now back off, Dylan. Back off!"

Dylan logrolled his body out of the frame as if someone had thrown a cherry bomb his way. Then he looked up. It was beautiful. He saw the scarf trailing in the wind, the cigar sticking out beneath Jaws's curled lip, the glittering earring, the now-empty Bugs Bunny glass with its straw, the radio, the green umbrella with its fringe dangling.

Jaws heard the camera click too. At once he jumped from his hole, pawing over the table to get to Amy. The umbrella fell like a shattered mast. Dylan clambered to his feet and followed, "Did you get it? Did you get it?" he yelled.

Amy slung the camera back over her shoulder and threw her arms around the excited Jaws. "Good boy," she said. "You were super." Then she turned to Dylan, her palm out flat. "Give me five," she said.

Dylan slapped her hand. He nuzzled his cheek against Jaws's head and felt the dog's tongue on his face. "We did it," he said. "We did it!"

TWELVE

DYLAN SAT WITH his knees up, his back resting against the drugstore's brick front. He thought he was crazy for hanging out here at this time of day. Max and the guys were probably flipping for quarters this very second. Today was a meeting day. Almost every Mighty Four meeting ended with a late-afternoon video bash at the arcade. Turning the sand dollar over in his hand, Dylan shaded his eyes and looked up the street again. The delivery van was nowhere in sight.

"Okay, here's the poop," Amy said, giving the page of figures she had been working on a sharp rap. She was wearing the white-framed plastic sunglasses she had found on the beach. The ones with GET UGLY stenciled in one corner. Dylan thought the glasses made her look cool.

"We've got eight sure places," Amy continued. "We could start out with ten cards in each place. Even if we only sold half of them, we'd more than make up our investment. Pretty safe bet, wouldn't you say?"

Dylan eyed the scrawled numbers. Those written by the lady at the print shop leaned to the right; Amy's slumped left. It looked as though a flock of sandpipers had trotted over the page. "*If* the picture comes out," he warned. "You said yourself that photographers never count their pictures before they're developed."

Amy whipped off her glasses. She raised her arms heavenward and rolled her eyes so that only the whites showed. She looked like Moses about to part the Red Sea. "No faith," she said dramatically. "The kid's got no faith."

Dylan laughed. "I can't help it. This waiting is getting to me."

Amy sighed and nodded. She shot an anxious glance up the street. Dylan craned his neck for a look too. Still no van. Amy began tapping her pencil on the sidewalk. The tapping got faster and faster. "Give me that!" she said suddenly, grabbing the sand dollar and cupping it in her hands. She jiggled the shell and blew on it like a gambler pleading with a pair of dice.

Dylan smiled.

"Don't say a word, Dylan Robertson. I'm just covering all bases. If that picture doesn't come out, it will take us days to get back to this point again."

They were on their feet long before the van came to a stop. Half the painted letters advertising CITIZEN PHOTO disappeared from the side of the van as the woman driver threw open the sliding door. She hauled out a cardboard box and walked briskly into the store, a clipboard sandwiched under one arm. Amy blew on the sand dollar one last time before handing it back to Dylan. The woman came out a minute later, the clipboard swinging at her side.

"Did it come?" Amy shouted at the clerk. "Gallagher . . . G-A-L . . ."

"I know, I know," the man said. He took the lid off the box and flipped through the envelopes like a librarian rifling through a card catalog.

"Let's see. E . . . F . . . G . . . Gallagher, Amy. Yep, it's here. Must be pretty important, eh?"

"Top secret," Amy said, grasping the packet and hugging it to her chest.

"That'll be six-fifty."

Dylan unrolled the two five-dollar bills and stuck his hand out for the change. They ran to the little park near the antiques shop and plopped down on one of the benches.

"Here, you'd better do it," Amy said. "I've got the heebies."

Dylan ripped open the envelope and took out the prints. On top was the picture of him that first day at the café. "I look mad," he said.

"You *were* mad. I thought you were going to bite my head off."

Dylan flipped through the pictures. There was the one of him and Jaws on the beach, a few of Amy's grandparents working in the garden, a whole series of the tree frog taken the day of the stakeout, and some town shots. Then there it was. Jaws in all his splendor. Looking like a sun-soaked tourist enjoying a day at the beach. Bugs Bunny glass and all.

"It's wonderful!" Amy said, yanking Dylan's hands over for a closer look. "I was so worried about it being out of focus. But it's perfect!"

"I can't believe it," Dylan said, shaking his head. "It's . . ." He stopped, his body racked with a feverish giggle. "People will go crazy for it."

"A title!" Amy cried. "We need a title."

Dylan leapt up. He closed his eyes to shut out everything but Jaws's image and the phrases that were orbiting his brain: BEACH DOG. GREETINGS FROM SEAVIEW. FUN IN THE SUN. WHAT A LIFE.

"Seaview," he yelled. "It's a Dog's Life!"

His eyes opened wide.

"Oh," Amy said in the lowest of tones. She crouched down like a dancer coiling before a jump. Then she sprang up. "That is just BRILLIANT!"

Dylan took a row of shrubs in front of the print shop like a champion high-hurdler. The sound of the bike engine coming from Mr. Bronski's lot made him lift his hands as though pulling up on handlebars. The imaginary front tire spun a slow circle in the air before him. When his feet touched the ground, he could feel the back tire spitting up earth as it dug for traction. "Yeah," he whispered.

*

There was a strange car parked in front of the cottage when Dylan arrived home. The car looked old, like the ones advertised on the yellowed calendars on the back wall of Mr. Bronski's shop. It was sleek and pudgy-looking at the same time. A shiny chrome ornament of a man with a winged helmet jutted from the hood. Dylan poked his head inside the open window. The car smelled of well-worn upholstery, and of something vaguely familiar.

"How do you like my wheels?" Aunt Jolene boomed as Dylan pushed open the screen door. "Oh, poor child, you look as if you've seen a ghost. It's just me. I had a couple days off and thought I'd drive my new buggy up this way and surprise you and your mom."

Aunt Jolene winked at Dylan. "Think you can put me up for a few days? I need a vacation from that desert heat. I was starting to feel like a mummy down there. Horrifying, really. People walking around like dried-out prunes. One of the hottest summers on record. Well, don't tell me you're too old to give your aunt a hug."

Dylan rushed over and threw his arms around her. She smelled of roses; it was the scent he had noticed in the car. He was glad Aunt Jolene hadn't changed perfumes. Dylan hadn't seen his mother's older sister in two years—not since the last time she had dropped in when they were living in Coleville.

"I got a phone call at work," his mother said. "Jo wanted to know if we had any plans for supper." She laughed.

"I always figure it's best not to give anyone advance warning," Aunt Jolene said. "That way they can't tell me to forget it."

"The car is great," Dylan said. "Will you take me for a ride sometime?"

Aunt Jolene smiled. "I was hoping you'd be my chauffeur. You do have your driver's license, don't you? Been such a long time. I was afraid you might have taken to the open road in search of your fortune. How old are you now, anyway . . . sixteen? Seventeen?"

"Please, Jo," Dylan's mother said. "Don't age the boy before his time. Next thing you know you'll have him married off."

"Not me," Dylan said, a little embarrassed. He turned and peered out at the car again. "What year is it?"

"Nineteen hundred and forty-nine. I just couldn't resist. Your uncle thought I'd gone off my rocker when I brought it home. Donald says I'm getting more eccentric as I get older. I tell him it's because he's made me live in that hot sun for so many years. Fried brains, you know. But I love him anyway. Poor thing."

Dylan told all about Amy and Jaws and the postcards over supper.

"I'd like to meet that girl," Aunt Jolene said. "And that photogenic dog too. Sounds like they're right up my alley."

"I think Dylan is saving Amy all for himself," Dylan's mother said. "Even I haven't been introduced yet."

After supper, they piled into the old Chevy and headed for the beach. The seats were soft and cushiony, the engine quiet and solid. Nothing like the pickup.

Dylan stayed in the car while the two women went for a walk. He figured he could walk on the beach any old time. He climbed over the seat and slid into the driver's place, wrapping his fingers around the thick ivory-colored steering wheel. Using the chrome man with the winged helmet as his guide, he turned the wheel this way and that, as though speeding around the snaky curves of the Coast Highway.

When he got tired of that, Dylan took out the road atlas from the glove compartment. He opened it to the big map in front with all the states. He found Chicago and calculated the distance between there and Seaview. Nearly two-thousand miles. Amy had sure come a long way. Then he checked California and found Bakersfield, where Aunt Jolene lived. That was pretty far away too. Everything seemed to be far from Seaview. The country was so big. How could anyone ever see it all?

Dylan decided he would try to see as much as he could when he grew up. He was going to go everywhere, do everything. And he would take his mother places too. If she wanted to go. Maybe they'd go to Vermont, or Texas, or even Alaska. What the heck, you only live once, as Aunt Jolene liked to say.

"What about me?"

It was his father's voice.

"You stay out of this," Dylan told the voice. "We'll send you a postcard. MAYBE. If we know what jail you're in."

Damn.

The women returned, laughing, arm in arm, and Aunt Jolene suggested they drive around some of the nearby streets. "I want to get a feel for this town," she said. Dylan scootched up alertly when one of the turns brought them onto Lupine Street. He yelled for Aunt Jolene to stop when he saw Amy and Jaws on the Gallaghers' front porch. He waved and watched the surprise blossom over Amy's face. She ran for the car with Jaws barking at her heels.

"So that's the soon-to-be-famous dog?" Aunt Jolene said. "Looks like a real star."

Mr. Gallagher appeared around the side of the house to see what all the excitement was about. "This sure takes me back," he said, pointing at the car with his pruning shears. "I used to have a car just like this. I won't say how many years ago, but it's been a while." He held out his hand. "I'm Amy's grandfather, Tom Gallagher. Pleased to meet you both."

The grown-ups continued talking, and Amy stuck her head inside the car. "Wow," she told Dylan. "Looks like a bigwig's car. A mobster's, or a movie star's, or something."

"That's because it's old," Dylan said. "And because of the new paint job."

"Boy, String Bean would go ape over a car like this," she said. "He's always talking about getting a real old car when he gets his license. One with class. He'd sure be a hit at school with a car like this."

It was getting dark. Aunt Jolene flicked on the headlights. Dylan and Amy repeated their plans to pick up the cards the next day. Then they all said good-bye.

"Nice folks," Aunt Jolene said on the way home. "You should invite Amy over sometime before I leave. We could play some cards together. Crazy Eights. You still play Crazy Eights, don't you?"

But Dylan was hardly listening. He had his window rolled all the way down, letting the air bang against his face. He pictured himself guiding the old Chevy into the Seaview Elementary parking lot. When he eased the car to a stop, he was immediately mobbed by kids wanting a ride.

"Just wait your turn," he had to say. "One at a time. You'll all get a chance."

"Hey!" he heard an angry voice say. It was Max, looking as snobby as ever. "I get to go first," Max said. "My dad's the president of the bank, remember?"

Dylan stuck his thumb out the window and snapped back his wrist. "The line starts at the back, old buddy," he told the disappointed Max. Then Jake Motta got in, and Dylan stepped on the gas and circled the parking lot just as smooth as could be.

"You sure told him," Jake said with a snicker.

Dylan waited for a car to pass before swinging the Chevy onto the street. "You've got to let guys like Max know which end's up," he said, casually shifting into second.

". . . sounded pretty awful to me," Aunt Jolene was saying as the headlights swept across the blistered face of the COZY CABINS sign. She braked the car to a stop behind the pickup. "Would have driven me crazy."

"That was then," Dylan's mother said. "Doesn't seem nearly as bad now."

Dylan rolled up his window. "What doesn't?"

Aunt Jolene got out and held the seat for him. "Lost in space, huh? I'll bet you've got your first million from the cards already spent."

"I wasn't thinking about that," he said.

"Try thinking about your bike," his mother called from the cottage door.

Dylan picked the bike off the ground and wheeled it to its place along the side of the house. He went around to the back to see if Mo was out. A beam of yellow suddenly shot through the window screen as the kitchen light snapped on. Dylan heard his mother and Aunt Jolene move into the room. Aunt Jolene was whispering. She chuckled.

"A real dreamer, sometimes," his mother said. "Just like his father."

Dylan's reply was as swift as a bee's sting—his words shattering the night like a fist propelled through a window: "I am NOT like my FATHER!"

THIRTEEN

THE DRUGSTORE HAD the largest selection of cards in town. The big rack stood halfway down the side wall, separating the vitamins from the underarm sprays. Dylan counted out ten cards from the printshop box and handed them to Amy.

"Now, don't look," Amy said.

Dylan stood behind her as she fitted the cards into the empty slot the store manager had assigned them. She gave the rack a push and stepped aside. "Okay!"

Colors and shapes blended into a blur. The clicking sounds became squeaks as the heavy rack slowed. Finally the squeaking stopped. Dylan's stomach fluttered with pride and excitement.

There it was. Between a seascape and a photo of the state park. Jaws. In living color. Looking like a happy vacationer who's just knocked off a nice cold drink on a hot summer day. Lips curled around the cigar as if smiling. Head cocked as though listening to the music blaring from the radio. At the very top of the card, in large cursive lettering, was Dylan's caption—SEAVIEW . . . IT'S A DOG'S LIFE.

Amy giggled for the hundredth time. Then she drew back, looking at the card with a professional eye. "You were right," she said. "The pink beret and the red scarf *are* brutal together. Totally. Wait till my parents see it. Even String Bean will be proud when he finds out how I've launched my career."

Dylan tucked the box of cards under his arm. "Come on," he said. "I'll buy you a 7-Up at Mr. B.'s. I can't wait to show him. And Mrs. Allioto said she's saving a place for them on her rack. She wants them hot off the press too."

Suddenly three white-shirted boys moved into position and blocked the aisle. The shirts had MIGHTY THREE emblazoned on them with black marker.

Max stepped forward, baring his teeth in a grotesque grin. The new cap was clearly visible, its snow-white color calling attention to itself between the duller white of the surrounding teeth. Max raised a fist. His index finger popped up, switchblade-style, and pointed at the new tooth.

Dylan shrank back. Travis heaved his bulk forward and ripped the box from Dylan's side. Dylan lunged to retrieve it.

"Just hold on," Travis said.

"You give that back," Amy hissed.

Travis opened the box and took out one of the cards. "Not bad," he said, his hard face softening into a half smile. He held out the card to the other boys.

Kevin read the caption out loud. His smile was cut short as Max shot him a stony glance. "Cute," Kevin spat. "Real cute."

Dylan's fists tightened at his sides. "Why can't you guys mind your own business? No one's doing anything to you. Just leave us alone."

"Just leave us alone!" Max mimicked. "Okay, baby. Here are your silly cards."

He grabbed the box from Travis and shoved it hard into Dylan's stomach. Dylan buckled with the pain. He recovered quickly and made a move toward Max, but Travis and Kevin both stepped forward at the same time to show that any attack on Max would be met by the whole group.

Max tore the card from Kevin's hand and crumpled it slowly, watching Dylan and Amy for their reactions. Dylan's eyes became slits. He felt Amy's hand on his arm, holding him back. "No, don't," she warned. "Not here. Let's not play his ugly game." She stared at Max. "Okay, you big hulk. That will be fifty cents."

For a moment Max seemed confused. Then he shrugged and drew out two quarters from his pocket. He flipped the quarters one after the other in Amy's direction. The coins landed on the floor, and Dylan watched them roll on their ends before falling flat near his feet. Neither he nor Amy made a move to pick them up.

"Just to let you know that I pay for what I take," Max said. "Not like somebody's old man."

"What about the newspapers you wrecked?" Amy shot back.

"WHO ARE YOU ACCUSING?" Max shouted.

The words ripped through the quiet of the store like rifle fire. Dylan saw the young mother at the HALF OFF table reach for her daughter's hand. "Good grief," someone said from the next aisle over.

"Hey, what's going on back there?" the clerk behind the front counter called. The old woman he was waiting on turned to squint her displeasure. "You kids take care of your business and clear out," the clerk said. "We don't allow loitering."

"Yes, sir . . . sorry, sir . . . no loitering here, sir," Max said.

Travis and Kevin snickered.

The man glared. Dylan feared he would call the manager. He was relieved when the clerk went back to ringing the old woman's sale. He waited till he was sure all other eyes had turned from them. Then he told Max, "You know darn well you wrecked those papers last week."

"Do you have any idea what this twerp is talking about?" Max asked Travis and Kevin.

"Not me."

"What papers?"

Max squared his shoulders and stuffed the crumpled card into his back pocket. "Let's get out of here," he said. "We've wasted enough time with these dodo birds." The three turned around and swaggered toward the door. "Nice day," Max called to the clerk with a polite wave.

"Ooooh!" Amy said when they had left. "That bunch makes my skin crawl."

Dylan had to take a deep breath to calm his anger before he could speak. "Max has Kevin and Travis eating out of his hand. They think he's a god or something."

"He's a little tyrant is what he is," Amy replied.

Dylan looked at her. He had caught the fear in her voice. "Don't worry," he said. "I won't let them ruin this for us."

But he had no idea what he could do to prevent it.

*

The next night Dylan lay perfectly still on the sofa that was his bed while Aunt Jolene was visiting. He had the desire to scratch the new mosquito bite on his leg but held off, straining instead to catch the whispered words of his aunt coming from the kitchen.

"I just can't imagine staying in this town and having to put up with the results of Ed's foolishness. I know small towns. The talk and ugliness after something like this burns like wildfire. I'm surprised you haven't already taken me up on my offer. Bakersfield is a whole state away. You'd get used to the desert, and you could start again . . . fresh and clean."

There was a silence then, and Dylan could tell that his mother was searching for something to say.

"I know it's crazy, Jo. But Ed needs me. He's all alone."

"And why shouldn't he be?" Aunt Jolene replied. "Look what he's done. Don't get me wrong. I don't hate the man. Never have. But I always sensed he'd come to no good. He's not the patient kind. One scheme after another. This timber business is his third run-in with the law. You've put up with enough. Let him sit and stew in his own soup. Serves him right. You've got yourself to think about. And Dylan. Surely it hasn't been easy for him. The boy needs a better example than what Ed can provide."

Dylan listened to the soft sounds of his own breathing. He opened his eyes, and his gaze fell on the space on the wall where the picture of him and his dad had been. His mother hadn't said anything about the picture after that night. She had just taken it down.

There was a scraping of chairs, followed by the loud thumping of pipes that signaled that the water had been turned on.

"Honey, you can't stay here. The place is falling apart. Don't do it to yourself."

Then Dylan heard the sounds of his mother's sobs. And Aunt Jolene's quiet comforting: "There now. I don't mean to be cruel. It's just that you're my sister. And I love you and Dylan very much."

If his father had been close by at the time, Dylan would have slugged him. He would have hit his own father.

The mosquito bite on his leg came alive again. He scratched until he felt the warm, liquid feel of blood. Then he buried his head in his pillow, not wanting to hear anymore. Wanting only to sleep and to dream of Bakersfield or some other place far away.

He had an image of a large city. Chicago. And a house—small, but new and clean. And when he looked out the window of the house, he could see a tall, thin boy shooting baskets in the next-door neighbor's driveway. And a girl with a pink beret playing leap-frog with a black Lab.

FOURTEEN

DYLAN HEARD BIRDS when he awoke the next morning. It was like waking up in the tent that morning at Lost Lake. There must have been a thousand birds chirping all at once in the meadow where they had camped. He and his father had thrown on their trunks and raced each other down to the lake. They'd swum clear out to the middle, and Dylan climbed onto his father's back.

"You're a sea monster, Dad! Give me a ride."

The monster swam with smooth strokes and made bubbling sounds. When they could touch bottom again, they took turns diving through each other's legs. On one dive, his father lifted Dylan all the way out of the water. Dylan shrieked with laughter. He clamped his legs around his dad's waist, threw his arms around the muscular neck. He felt ten-feet-tall as his father walked him in to shore.

Later, with their skin still tingling from the water, they'd made breakfast. Dylan learned how to make hobo coffee by throwing the grounds into a pot of boiling water. They made biscuits too, baking them in an oven of glowing coals. There was the smell of bacon as it popped in the frying pan, the sizzle of the eggs as they hit the hot grease. His father kept shaking his head and saying, "This is the life, huh, son?" And Dylan could hardly stand it . . . the taste of honeyed biscuits in his mouth, his father's wide grin . . . and birds. Birds everywhere!

When the sleep finally cleared from his head, Dylan realized he was hearing the chirping melody of flute music. The radio had been turned up loud. His mother and Aunt Jolene were using the kitchen as a runway as they darted between their rooms and the bath, getting ready for the trip to Rockport.

Dylan packed the cooler in the trunk and waited by the car. He used his shirt to rub at a water spot on the passenger door. He had washed the old Chevy the night before so it would look its best.

"Shoes!" his mother said when she came out and saw his bare feet.

"But it's going to be hot."

"I doubt you have anything to worry about. Those sneakers of yours are well-enough ventilated."

Dylan frowned and hurried back inside.

"Okay?" he asked when he returned.

"Ugh," his mother said, making a face at the shoes. "He goes through them like paper," she told Aunt Jolene. "Don't think I haven't offered to get him a new pair. But he insists they're fine for the summer."

It wasn't a lie. His mother *had* offered, but they had both agreed it would be a good idea to wait till school started. It would be more important to look good for school, and Dylan knew his mother's paycheck didn't stretch very far.

"Look fine to me," Aunt Jolene said. "Air-conditioned, right?"

"Right," Dylan replied as he climbed into the backseat.

Aunt Jolene tooted once as she turned into the Gallaghers' driveway. Amy shot out the door, dressed in yellow shorts and a matching top. "Hi, you all," she said, swinging her pack into the car.

Mrs. Gallagher ran from the house, a sweater clutched in her hand. "Wait," she said. "It gets windy there by the water. You'd better take this, just in case."

She stepped back with a sigh, her faced lined with worry. "Now, you be careful," she instructed. Dylan thought the warning was as much for Aunt Jolene as for Amy.

"No need to fret," Aunt Jolene said. "This ancient buggy has only one speed—slow. Besides, we want to enjoy the scenery. I plan to take it nice and easy."

Mrs. Gallagher dipped her head in an unsure nod. She struggled for a smile.

"We'll be back long before dark," Dylan's mother said.

"Whew!" Amy said after waving good-bye one last time. "Gram's been telling me to be careful ever since we got up. I thought you'd never get here." She leaned over to Dylan and whispered close to his ear. "Do you know what she said? She said that I shouldn't get too close to the prison because someone might be trying to escape, and the guards might have to shoot. Can you bear it?"

Dylan didn't laugh. He had been trying to put the prison part of the trip out of his mind. He knew the main reason for the trip was so Aunt Jolene and his mom could visit his father. It was only when his mother suggested that he invite Amy, and when Aunt Jolene thought of a picnic, that he had agreed to go. He and Amy would wait outside in the car. The visit wouldn't take that long. With Amy there, Dylan knew it would be all right.

"I hope you pulled the door shut when you went for your shoes," his mother said as they passed the cottage.

"So that's where you live," Amy said, stretching her neck for a better look.

Dylan kept his eyes straight ahead. He caught a glimpse of the sign with the metal gull spinning crazily in the wind. He hadn't looked at the gull much lately. Suddenly his father's words came back to him. "Maybe that bird *will* fly someday . . . just biding its time."

Well, Dylan thought, even if his mother did decide to wait for his father, to continue to be married to a thief, he wouldn't have to stick around to see it. In a few months he'd be thirteen. He'd have the trail bike by then. Lots of kids ran away when they were thir-teen.

He could see himself zooming over back roads, spending his nights in little county parks, getting odd jobs here and there. He could pick fruit in the summer and fall and learn how to prune the trees in the spring. The winter?—well, he didn't know about that yet. Maybe someone nice would take him in if he prom-ised to do chores and help out. There were lots of ranches in the eastern part of the state. He was used to a tiny closet of a room. And he certainly didn't eat much.

"Dylan! Are you deaf?"

Amy's elbow peppered his side.

"I said we sold three more cards at the drugstore. Gramps and I walked there early this morning for a Sunday paper. That's five cards in two days. In just one place. We'll be rich!"

Yes, that's good, Dylan thought. But he couldn't quite get the words out.

Amy gave him a look that said he was impossible. She scooted forward, crossing her arms over the seat. "Sometimes I don't understand boys," she said. "String Bean—that's my brother—he made the honor roll last year. Only twenty-five kids out of two hundred made it, and it hardly fazed him at all. It was like he'd been told he had the mumps or something. But when Alicia Thompson called him one night, he went bananas. He did a cartwheel out the door. Jogged ten blocks and back. Just because of a phone call."

"Sounds like old String Bean was in love," Aunt Jolene said.

Amy filled her cheeks with air and blew. "I guess that was it," she said. "But *Alicia Thompson*? You should see her on the bus in the morning. She'd trample over a class of preschoolers to get a boy's attention. I could have told String Bean that it wouldn't work. But he's a slow-learner when it comes to commonsense things. He and Alicia ended up going steady for all of six days and three-and-a-half hours."

Dylan joined in the laughter.

"I hear your parents are in Europe for a vacation," his mother said to Amy a few moments later.

Amy nodded. "They needed a break from us kids. Dad jumped at the opportunity even though he's been sick lately. He said he'd have a lot better chance resting up in Paris or Rome than at our house."

"I hope he's not seriously ill," Aunt Jolene said.

"Not now. But the doctor says his heart isn't in too good a condition. He's a lot older than Mom."

They were quiet, then, as the car turned a bend in the road and the ocean sparkled through a gap in the trees.

"Of course he's not my real father," Amy added when the ocean disappeared again. "But I love him just the same. Even more."

Dylan's ears perked to attention. He had never dreamed that Amy had a stepfather. He had assumed that everything about Amy would be completely normal. He wondered if her first father was a skunk, or an okay guy. Or which of the two she took after. Maybe her real father was also a criminal, and he had run away because the FBI was on his trail. Then the thought crossed his mind that maybe Amy's real father was dead. And he felt sorry for her. Just as he sometimes felt sorry for himself. As far as he was concerned, his father was dead too.

An hour later they turned off the highway and drove away from the ocean. The air was sweet with ripening blackberries and corn. A flock of gulls busily scratched a newly plowed field for worms. Everything seemed peaceful. Then, boom. Dylan felt his whole body go hot. The big stone prison sat on the hill up ahead like a dragon-monster overlooking its domain. Waiting to gobble up anyone who came near.

FIFTEEN

UP CLOSE, THE PRISON didn't look like a dragon at all. More like an old, run-down castle. High walls surrounded the main building. There was barbed wire strung across the tops of the walls and a tower at each corner. The towers were notched with little window-holes. Dylan saw a man with a gun standing atop the right tower. Two men in uniform stood by the main gate. They looked bored. Dylan couldn't tell if they wore pistols or not.

Aunt Jolene parked in the middle of an empty row of spaces. A stand of tall poplar trees separated the parking lot from the road. Across the road was a small, fenced-in cemetery, all green.

When they got out of the car, Dylan's mother held up the mirror of her compact and hurriedly brushed her hair. Then she took a package out of the trunk. She sometimes brought treats on her visits. Cheeses and nuts and cookies and things. "We won't be long," she said. "You two stick close."

She stared at Dylan with a questioning look. Dylan looked away. "Okay," she said to Aunt Jolene. "Let's go."

Dylan leaned against the car. The mosquito bite on his leg had scabbed over, but it still itched. He tossed his head back to clear the bangs from his eyes. Squinting, he saw that his mother and Aunt Jolene had stopped at the gate. The men stationed there said something to them. Then one of the men wrote on his clipboard and waved them through.

"What's it like?" Amy said.

"What's what like?"

"The prison. I mean, inside."

"How would I know?"

"You mean you've never been?"

He turned away, exhaling an angry snort through his nose. "Why would I want to go inside a jail?" he said.

"I just thought—"

"Look, it's too hot here," he broke in. "I'm boiling over. Let's go over there where it's shady."

They crossed the road, jumped the cemetery's low fence, and walked till they came to a large open area with a big pine tree in the middle. Dylan sat down in the shade of the tree while Amy threaded her way among the surrounding tombstones.

"Look at this one," Amy called. She pointed to a stone that was cut in the shape of a car. "DEWEY MORRISON. BORN JULY 17, 1904—DIED APRIL 5, 1979. MAY THE STREETS OF HEAVEN BE PAVED FOR DRIVING."

"Pretty corny," Dylan said.

"Yeah, but it's original. Think I'll get a shot of it. He must have been a race-car driver or something. Wonder if he's got a little model car buried with him. That's what the Egyptians did. They were buried with model sailing ships to take them to the afterworld. They believed you had to cross a river in order to get there, so they made sure they had a ship."

"Sounds pretty dumb," Dylan said. "How'd they expect to cross a river with a toy ship?"

"Hmmm," Amy said. "Never thought of that."

She took a picture, then strolled back to the tree. "Want to explore some? The land drops off in the back there. I thought I heard a creek."

Dylan frowned. "Too hot for running around."

Amy sat down cross-legged beside him. She picked a few blades of grass and started weaving them together. "Something eating you?" she asked.

He knew he hadn't been doing a real good job of hiding it. "I was just wondering," he said. "Is your father still alive? I mean, your real father."

"As far as I know. The last any of us heard, he was in Louisiana working on a fishing boat. He left when I was three. I hardly remember him."

"Do you look like him?"

"Mom says I've got his eyes. And I guess my curly hair comes from Dad too, since Mom's is more wavy than curly. Why?"

Dylan figured if he got his hair cut short and grew a mustache, he'd look just like his dad. Maybe that was why he had been putting off getting a haircut.

He had even noticed a little fuzz starting to sprout on his upper lip and had thought of using his mother's razor to shave it off. He held his hands out in front of him. At least his fingers were long and thin like his mother's. That was some consolation.

"Well," he said, "do you act like your father? Your real father, I mean."

Amy shrugged. "How do I know? I told you he left when I was three. I'm certainly not planning on running away to Louisiana and hitching up with a fishing boat, if that's what you mean."

She gave up on the weaving and flung the blades of grass to the ground. Dylan sighed. She looked at him. "Mom says I've got a bit of Dad's love for the outdoors and travel," she said. "Does that help?"

Dylan felt his stomach sink. "So you are like your real father, then? I mean you look like him a little, and you like being outdoors and traveling."

"So what? A lot of people like to travel and be outdoors. Look at my stepdad. He's running around Europe this very minute. No, I don't think I'm like any of them, really. Not even Mom. Mom's skin is so silky-smooth people can't help staring. And she hates taking pictures. She buys postcards and already-made slides so she doesn't have to mess with a camera. She also thinks Jaws is a nuisance a lot of the time. I think he's one of the best things that ever happened."

Dylan recalled what his mother had said of him the night they had stopped at Amy's. "A real dreamer, sometimes. Just like his father." But didn't his mother dream too? Didn't everyone? And that commercial he had seen on TV . . . about the dangers of smoking. There was a man and a boy. The man was lighting up, and the boy looked like he thought it was the cool thing to do. "Like father, like son," the announcer had said.

Well, he thought. Maybe it didn't have to be that way. Maybe Amy was right. You might have to look like your parents because, after all, they made you. No getting around that. But who said you had to *be* like them?

Suddenly Amy was overtaken by a fit of laughter.

"What?"

"Gramps!" she howled. "He said there wasn't another person like me in the whole entire world. That was when he saw me brushing Jaws's teeth before we took the picture. He just threw up his hands when he said it. Only thing was, he had a cup of flour in his hand at the time. The flour landed—plop—all over Gram's begonias. We had a heck of a time cleaning it up before Gram got out of the shower."

She went on smiling, as if replaying the scene another time in her head. "You know, it's kind of neat to think that you're one of a kind. That's why I like old Dewey Morrison's stone over there. It's one of a kind. And I'll bet he thought of that too. Before he died, that is,"

As Dylan listened to Amy, whatever had been eating him seemed to have gotten its fill. He breathed deeply, his chest rising with the pine-scented air.

They spent the rest of the time thinking up funny, one-of-a-kind tombstones for people they knew. Amy's brother's would be a carved pair of stilts with a string bean across the top. Dylan thought of a giant tooth with freckles for Max—and a couple of huge M&M's for Travis. They decided that Amy's grandfather's would be a statue of him with a hoe in hand, stepping on a slug.

"A squirrel for Leslie Morganti," Amy said, *tsk*ing loudly and rolling her eyes.

"Mrs. Allioto's would have to be a burger," Dylan laughed. "With everything on it."

Amy thought hers would be a camera. "With chocolate lip prints," she said. "In honor of my victory over Freddie Maldoon. What about you?"

"A trail bike, of course," Dylan said right away. Then he added, "With a sea gull riding on it."

He wasn't sure why he thought of it that way. The two just seemed to go together somehow.

SIXTEEN

THE NEXT WEEK was almost too good to be true. Mrs. Allioto said the postcard of Jaws had become her biggest seller overnight. Even the photo-card of the sun setting behind Haystack had fallen to second place behind Jaws at the café.

"That dog is *hot*," Mr. Bronski said. "Better get yourselves another batch printed up pronto. The card is so dang funny, people can't resist it."

"It's like somebody added yeast to the thing," Dylan told Amy on Friday. He was talking about the mason jar in his dresser drawer. "I have to keep punching the dollar bills down to make room."

Amy was just as excited. "Every store owner is saying to keep 'em coming. We've got a gold mine on our hands. I might even start checking prices on camera lenses. Mom says smart shoppers start early."

"How's Jaws?" Dylan asked.

"He's in Dog Heaven. He's the only dog in the world who gets to look forward to a dish of bubble-gum ice cream every night after his Alpo."

Dylan sighed happily. "And no Max and the gang. I don't understand it. I thought for sure they'd try to ruin it for us. You saw what Max was like at the drugstore."

"He's a windbag," Amy scoffed. "Even windbags get tired of blowing air."

To celebrate their luck, Dylan suggested that they rent a bike from Mr. Bronski.

"You're on," Amy said. "I was hoping we could do something really special before D-Day."

D-Day was Amy's term for Departure Day. Two days earlier she had received a letter from her parents saying that they would be coming home on schedule. Her grandmother had already called the airport to confirm Amy's flight reservation.

Dylan hadn't given much thought to D-Day. It was still nearly two weeks away. But now that Amy had mentioned it, he thought it was sort of like having a splinter in your hand. Not a big one, just a tiny fleck of a thing. Most of the time you don't even remember the sliver is there. Then you suddenly notice it, and you say, "Oh, yeah, that."

*

On Saturday, Dylan met Amy and Jaws at Mr. Bronksi's. It was a blue-sky day. Nothing but sunshine. Mr. B. took them out back to the practice track. He had Amy drive around and around until she had a good feel for the bike. Dylan took a few circles too. The bike was just like the one he had ridden with his father, and it didn't take him long to get the hang of it again.

"You shouldn't have any problems," Mr. B. said, giving the brim of his fisherman's cap a confident tug. "You'll have to walk the bike to the beach, since you're not old enough to ride the streets. Stay on the hard sand when you get there. And wear your helmets the whole time."

"I don't think this is what Mr. Bronski had in mind," Amy said a few minutes later. Her voice sounded faraway.

"I feel like an astronaut," Dylan said. He laughed.

They were strutting down the sidewalk with their helmets on, the spangly-new bike between them. The green-tinted face shields of the helmets acted like sunglasses. Jaws kept rushing up to them, then backing off.

"He's not sure what to make of us," Dylan said. "Maybe he feels left out. You want a helmet too, boy? . . . Wouldn't he look great in one? The world's first space dog."

Amy laughed. "Don't think I won't keep that idea on file."

The beach was stretched its widest with the low tide. Kids with shovels and sand pails were hard at work near the water's edge. A group of teenagers had their radio turned up full-blast to overcome the loud thunder of the surf. Jaws found a throwing stick and dashed over to a little boy who was skipping stones by himself.

They pointed the bike to the left. The southern expanse of beach was almost deserted. A half mile away, barely visible, was the driftwood fort of the Mighty Four. *Three,* Dylan mumbled under his breath.

"You drive first," Amy said as she hopped on the back of the soft, vinyl-covered seat.

Dylan straddled the bike. He turned the key to the ON position and pushed the starter button. The engine roared to life. He sat down and adjusted the mirrors, his sneakers reaching for the footrests. "Hang on," he said. Amy wrapped her arms around his waist. "Go for it!" she shouted.

The bike lurched as Dylan slowly turned the throttle handle toward him. He kept turning until the machine stopped its jerking and shot forward, the tires smoothly rolling over the hard sand. He opened it up even more. The back tire bit in. The engine roared louder. Amy tightened her grasp. "Faster!" she cried.

They reached top speed as Dylan's hand held the throttle open full-bore. The engine was really screaming now. The wind hummed around Dylan's helmet. He steered the bike in long, graceful curves, like a skier weaving down a course. He straightened the front tire as a small dark ribbon of water appeared ahead. The bike cut through the streambed. Water sprayed up, pattering his helmet, splashing his arms. Amy howled with delight.

Dylan applied the brakes as the headland zoomed closer. The engine shunted down through the gears.

The bike slowed, then came to a sudden stop, jerking them both forward.

"Whooo," Amy said. "That was the absolute greatest!"

They switched places. Amy steered the bike around in a wide, slow circle, then wrenched the throttle toward her. The bike answered her command, and they were sailing again.

Dylan had just settled back for the ride, when he saw something that made him shiver. Or at least he thought he saw it: a tiny patch of rippled blue above the driftwood fort far to his right. He swerved his head around for a second look. But by now the bike was well past the log fort. He trained his eyes on the quick-moving wooded bank for the rest of the ride, searching for parked bikes.

Worried, he told Amy to take his turn as driver when they reached the upper end of the beach. Amy looked as if someone had just awarded her a free trip to Disney World.

Dylan rode with his helmet off so he'd have a clearer view. He held on to Amy with one arm and leaned out over the bike when they passed the fort again. But there was no blue flag, no signal that a meeting of the Mighty Three was in session.

Jaws had followed the bike down. He came bounding up with the throwing-stick in his mouth, his tail pulsing.

Amy let the engine idle, and got off, flicking down the kickstand. "I haven't had this much fun since I almost lost my lunch on the Wild Mouse at Roseland Park," she said. "Talk about roller coasters!"

She bent down and gave Jaws a hug. "What'd you do, tire out that poor little boy already?" Then she took the camera from her pack. "Let me get a shot of you," she told Dylan. "An action shot for our scrapbook."

Dylan put his helmet back on and wheeled the bike around. "It'll go faster if just one person rides at a time," he said. "I'll take her down once on my own. Then you can."

Amy positioned herself a few yards down the beach. "Okay," she said. "Let it rip!"

The bike shrieked and reared like a spurred horse as Dylan yanked the throttle his way. He swung the bike toward the water, then steered a straight line through a long stretch of stranded foam. He bent down over the handlebars to gain even more speed. It would have been perfect, if not for the disturbing thoughts that kept poking around in his head. It bugged him that he had been so worried about Max and the gang. So what if they were having a meeting? Was he just plain chicken?

When the creek appeared, he aimed the bike for a high drift of sand on the near bank. He stood straight up as the bike arched up and over the sandy ramp. For a second, he was floating in midair, the tires spinning silently, his body shot-through with electricity. Then the back tire landed hard, the front tire slamming down a moment later. He had to hang on with all his might as the bike bucked and skidded before righting itself.

He continued up the beach, the moisture returning to his parched mouth. Not a bad jump, he thought, feeling the smile cross his face. Take *that*, Chicken Little.

*

"I think we might be moving," Dylan said as he and Amy sat in the shade of one of the honeycomb caves. Jaws lay between them, panting contentedly. They had left the bike on the other side of the headland and hiked around the rock wall as they had done that first time. Dylan had the key to the bike tucked safely in his pocket. It felt good to him being back at the caves after so long. Like reclaiming something that was rightfully his.

"Aunt Jolene's offered to put us up at her house in Bakersfield," Dylan added. "She thinks it'd be better for us to start over in someplace new."

"What does your mom think?"

"I don't know exactly. But she's been awful quiet since Aunt Jolene left. I can tell she's thinking hard about things, what with school coming up and all."

Amy scowled as she scooped another handful of sand over her legs. "Why do the summers go so fast? In a few weeks it'll be school this and school that. Worst of all, I'll be going to the new junior high. There'll be a couple thousand kids. We'll all be bumping into one another, checking our maps to find out where our next class is, or where the bathrooms are."

Although Dylan wasn't sure about moving to the desert, he certainly wasn't looking forward to going back to the same school where he'd have to face being called a convict's son again. "I still have to figure out something to do about Max and the guys," he said. "I know you think they've given up. But if Max were an animal, he'd be a weasel. I bet they're up at the pond right now. Swimming and scheming."

"How come we've never gone to the pond?" Amy asked. "Those dingbats don't own it, do they?"

"No."

"Well, it'd sure be nice to go swimming in water that doesn't turn your whole body purple for a change."

Dylan felt himself blush. "There's another reason why we've never gone up there," he said. "It's not just because of those three."

"You think my Australian crawl is *that* bad?"

He smiled. "No, it's because, well, no one really goes up to the pond but kids. Mostly boys. And when there're no girls around, which is pretty much always, the boys go skinny-dipping. You know, without swimsuits or anything."

Amy whistled. Then she laughed. "Imagine. All those bare bottoms running around. They'd probably all have heart attacks if a girl suddenly showed up. . . . You know, someone should do it. Free the pond for girls too. Someone . . . but not me," she quickly added. "Joan of Arc, I'm not."

Dylan had promised Mr. Bronski that they'd have the bike back by five, but he wanted to get some more riding in first. Amy led the way back around the rock cliff. Suddenly she shouted, "Dylan! Look!"

Dylan leapt the remaining six feet to the ground. He dashed to the bike. It stood leaning on its kickstand, right where they had left it. But it was lower now. The sand was high around the limp tires. Dylan's fingers found the holes in the back tire. He scrambled to the front. The front tire had been slashed too. He raced for the fort, charging like a madman. "They did it!" he screamed. "Come out, you cowards! You idiots!" He streaked into the fort. But there was no one there. Only the square blue flag, lying in a tumble on the sandy floor.

SEVENTEEN

MRS. GALLAGHER WAS beside herself. "I knew it," she cried to her husband. "I just knew something like this would happen. Tom! The police! And you just let her go."

Her eyes swung to Dylan. Dylan flinched backward with the force of the stare. It was like being gored by some sharp-horned animal.

"It's not Dylan's fault," Amy yelled. "He didn't do anything. It's those thugs. Max deserved to lose a tooth for what he said about Dylan's father. He's a brat!"

"The police," Mrs. Gallagher repeated softly to herself as if she had heard nothing. "You're just a baby. Your poor mother. What will she think?"

"I am *not* a baby!" Amy shouted. "And my mother has nothing to do with this."

"That's enough," Mr. Gallagher said. "How can I

136

get heads or tails of what's going on if everyone is yelling and screaming?"

Amy started again, slowly, from the beginning. This time Mrs. Gallagher didn't interrupt. Amy told how they had found the bike with its tires slashed, and how Dylan had seen the blue signal-flag earlier. She told about the threats Max, Travis, and Kevin had been making, and about how she and Dylan had pushed the injured bike back to the lot.

"What does Bronksi say about all this?" Mr. Gallagher asked when she had finished.

"He was real good about it," Amy said. "He said he knows we wouldn't do a thing like that. Why on earth would we? He called the police, and they filled out a report. They're going to talk to those nitwits."

Dylan found his voice. "Not that it'll do any good. They'll never admit to it."

"They might," Amy said hopefully. "Sometimes the police can be pretty persuasive."

Mrs. Gallagher wrung her hands. "How do *you* know, young lady? When's the last time you had to deal with the police over something like this?"

Amy groaned. "Never. But I've seen it on TV. They can tell when someone's guilty."

"This is *not* TV," Mrs. Gallagher snapped. "This is real. And you are implicated in a crime."

Dylan could see tears welling in Amy's eyes. "We have nothing to be ashamed of," he said, coming to her defense.

"Humph!" Mrs. Gallagher said.

"So what do you two plan to do about this?" Mr. Gallagher asked. "Since you rented the bike, you know that you're responsible for it."

"I know," Dylan said. He pictured the mason jar at home—empty. "Mr. B. said the tires will come to eighty dollars. I'll cover the cost with my savings."

"No!" Amy said. "We rented the bike together. Gramps, I'll have to borrow some money from you, if that's okay. But I promise to pay you back."

"Max has it in for me, not you," Dylan said. "You've got nothing to do with it. You shouldn't have to pay anything."

"But your savings! What about the bike you've been planning to buy?"

"There won't be any bike," he said sadly.

*

Dylan was expecting the worst. He thought the police would phone or send an officer over to question him some more. He had heard about the files they kept. Once they discovered his father was in prison, they might try to blame him for the bike even though Mr. Bronski had assured them that he and Amy were innocent. *Hey, that Dylan kid's father's a con,* they would say. *Do you suppose he's learned a few tricks from the old man?*

His mother was at the stove, still wearing her work overalls, the ones with the patches on the knees. Her hair was tied back with a scarf. She was humming, obviously pleased with her labors. "This place may be falling apart," she said, "but flowers make a big difference. I could kick myself for waiting so long."

For three days she had been busy building the planting boxes and putting up the shelves that would support them against the front of the cottage. Today she had transplanted marigolds and poppies into the planters. She was right. The flowers were a welcome splash of color against the peeling boards of the cottage. Dylan wondered if this meant they were staying for good. But the thought passed quickly. What had happened with the bike was a hundred times more important at the moment.

"You can at least try some of this eggplant," she told him halfway through supper.

"Mom, I've got something to tell you."

"Shoot," she said.

He spoke quickly, wanting to get it over with. When she finally replied, her words were crisp, her voice louder than usual.

"Two things. First, it won't do you any good to accuse anyone without proof. In fact, that can only make matters worse."

He was about to argue, but she shook her head.

"That's just one. The second is this. The next time you see Max, you should act as though everything is okay . . . no grudges, no accusations. If he did it, he might even feel badly enough to confess and pay his debt. Whatever possessed him to do such a thing—if he did—runs a lot deeper than losing the presidency of the Mighty Four. He's got a mean streak in him for some reason. But we've all got a little meanness in us. Just let it go."

"And let them get away with it?" Dylan cried.

"Love is mightier than the sword," she said.

Love! Dylan took his fork and speared a piece of eggplant. He threw the fork down on the table. "Love! I'll knock his block off. All three of them."

"No, you won't."

"I will!"

He leapt from his chair.

"Where are you going?"

"Out back."

"You stay right around here. You hear me?"

He threw himself down under one of the alders, feeling like a firebomb about to explode. So that's the way it is? Some people break the law and get away with it. Others get put into prison. No, his mother was wrong. She wanted him to lie down and play dead—like some coward. Those guys needed to be taught a lesson. This whole thing had gone on long enough. He was going to show them. And her.

Furious, he picked up a stick and snapped off the end. The new end was pointed. He jabbed the point hard into the ground like a sword. "Mightier than the sword," he scoffed, as his mother's words came back to him. Then he thought of Amy's T-shirt. THE PHOTOGRAPH IS MIGHTIER THAN THE SWORD. How dumb. How could a picture be mightier than a sword? It was only paper. Max and the others needed a good licking, not a photograph.

He was too mad to be scared. Tomorrow would be the day. He'd go to the fort. If they weren't there, he'd bike to the pond. He'd find them if he had to spend the whole day doing it.

The pond! The idea flashed like a neon sign inside him. The sign went blank. He waited for it to flash again. . . . Yes, yes, yes!

He barely saw his mother as he flew through the kitchen to the phone.

"I think we should talk some more about this," she called after him.

"Not now."

"Why not now?"

"Because!"

He dialed Amy's number and held his breath, hoping Mrs. Gallagher wouldn't answer.

"Hello."

"Amy, thank goodness. Listen. Can you get away tomorrow afternoon and meet me?"

"I don't know. Gram is hopping-mad. She said I'm not to see you, at least for a couple of days. She wants to think things through."

"It can't wait a couple days!"

"What can't?"

"My idea. I think I know how to work this all out, to fix those tire-slashers once and for all."

She hesitated. "I'm sorry about how Gram acted today. I know she hurt you."

"Never mind that now," he replied. "Meet me in front of Mr. B.'s at two. And bring your camera. It's our only chance."

"I'll be there," Amy said firmly.

Dylan put down the phone. His mother stood in the doorway, hands on hips, her head tilted in suspicion.

"What's up?"

"Nothing."

"Nothing?"

"Please," he said. "I'll fill you in as soon as I can. But it's bad luck to talk about something like this."

"Just promise me I won't have to bandage up any bruised faces tomorrow—yours or anybody else's."

He smiled for the first time since discovering the vandalized bike. "Mom, you know yourself, violence is never the answer."

"I'm waiting," she said, her foot tapping the floor in a no-nonsense manner.

"Okay," he said, "Cross my heart and hope to spit. I promise there'll be no need for bandages."

EIGHTEEN

DYLAN PACED THE sidewalk in front of Mr. Bronski's. It was so hot the soles of his sneakers were making little suction noises on the pavement. He checked the corner one more time. He was beginning to think that something had happened. It wasn't like Amy to be late.

Once again he found himself drawn to the fence that bordered the bike lot. His eyes focused past the wire mesh. The orange Honda was parked in its usual place. From this distance you couldn't even tell there were patches of rust on the gas tank. The faded orange paint looked fresh and new in the sun. "Some things are just plain tough," Mr. B. had said earlier when Dylan had handed over the eighty dollars.

Maybe so, Dylan thought. *But people can be tough too, and it's not over yet. Not by a long shot.*

Just then Amy turned the corner on her three-speed, with Jaws behind her.

"I made it," she said. "I had to tell Gramps. He said he'd cover for me. Remind me to pick up.a loaf of bread on the way home."

"Got your camera?"

"Always," she said, patting her back.

"I don't know about Jaws," Dylan said.

"But he wants to come."

"We're going to have to be real quiet."

"Oh, he'll be quiet," she said. "He's a hunting dog. Hunting dogs know when to be quiet."

Dylan wavered. Jaws sidled up and licked his ankle. "Okay," he said, remembering how Travis had called Jaws a mutt in front of the school that day. "I guess he's got a right to be in on this too."

"Good. Now, how about telling me what's going on."

"There'll be plenty of time on the way for that," Dylan said, reaching for his bike. "Let's go."

They rode east down Tillamook Street. The houses thinned when they passed the SEAVIEW THANKS YOU sign. The valley that stretched before them was a checkerboard of fields and farms. Ahead, the forested hills of the Coast Range jutted like shark's teeth into the sky.

Dylan turned onto a dirt road about a mile into the valley and stopped. "We'll hide our bikes down there," he said, pointing to where the road disappeared into a hillside of trees.

Amy thrust her hands on her hips. "I'm not going another foot unless you tell me what we're doing out here."

She stared pop-eyed when Dylan had finished laying out his plan. Dylan chuckled. "Better close your mouth," he said. "Lots of bugs around today."

"But you can't do this to me," she cried. "I'll crack under the pressure. I'll turn sky blue, pink, red, and scarlet all at the same time."

"You don't even have to look," Dylan said. "You can cover your eyes and look the other way. All you have to do is jump out at my signal."

Amy moaned.

"It'll all be over in a second," he added. "No sweat."

"Sure," she said. "The last time someone said those words to me, he had a six-inch needle in his hand. That tetanus shot hurt for a month."

Dylan lifted his hands. "No needles," he said.

Amy sucked in a deep breath. "Okay, but don't blame me if I faint dead away."

A rickety gate blocked the way where the road arched up sharply and the trees began. They hid their bikes in the brush off to the left, and Amy showed Dylan how to work the camera. "It's an automatic," she said. "All you have to do is point and press here." Then Dylan unlatched the gate's rusty wire, and they hurried through.

As they hiked up, Dylan prayed that the boys would be there. He had checked the fort earlier and had found it empty. He figured the chances were good they'd be up at the pond on one of the hottest days of the summer. Still, a chance was a chance. You could never be sure. His heart skipped a beat when he heard shouts and laughter up ahead.

Jaws's ears cocked to attention. He stood with one paw raised, his eyes fixed in the direction of the sounds.

"Easy, boy," Dylan said. "Hang on to him," he told Amy. "I'd better scout things out first."

He stepped from the road into the trees and crept forward, crouching low, and watching that he didn't step on any dry limbs. When he could see the pond's water sparkling between the tree trunks, he got down on all fours. He felt the blood pounding in the soft spots below his ears as he scuttled to safety behind one of the front-row trees.

The tree stood on the raised rim of ground that banked the circular pond. Dylan peered cautiously around the trunk. He had to keep himself from yelling out in triumph. To his left, the boys' bikes rose from the grassy bank like huge gleaming insects. On the narrow flat of dirt and stones at the water's edge were three piles of clothes and three pairs of sneakers.

Dylan looked out over the water. Max and Travis were hanging on to a floating log in the center of the pond. Kevin's head suddenly shot up out of the water beside them. The three boys laughed. Dylan watched as Max tried to sit on the half-submerged log. The log bucked and spun. Max's head and torso plunked into the water, his bare bottom trailing behind.

"We've struck gold!" Dylan said when he had backtracked to where Amy and Jaws were waiting.

Amy's face twisted into a pained expression. "Dylan, I can't. My legs have turned to jelly."

"You have to," he said. "It's the only way."

They tiptoed through the woods, with Amy keeping a firm hold on Jaws's collar so he wouldn't bolt away. At Dylan's signal, they hunched down and made their way to a shallow depression behind the pond's rim. Jaws whined to be free when he heard the shouts and splashing of the boys just a few yards away. Amy lifted his ear and whispered soothingly to him. Jaws seemed to forget about the shouts as he nuzzled Amy's face, his tail thumping the ground.

Dylan squiggled forward until his head reached just above the rim of the hollow. Amy followed. She had one eye closed as she poked her head over the top. She blew out a sigh when she realized they lay behind a clump of tall grass that blocked their view of the swimming boys.

"Crawl up after I leave, and stay low behind the grass," Dylan whispered. "Jaws will be all right with me."

Amy gulped. "I'll die. I know I'll die. You'd better come to my funeral. I want roses. Yellow ones."

Dylan smiled. "I'll be there with a cartload," he said. He slid Amy's pack onto his back. "Okay, boy," he told Jaws. "Surprise time."

Amy let go of the collar. Jaws barked and hurdled the lip of the hollow like a charging bull. Dylan climbed onto the bank. He tried striking a calm pose as he strode over to where the bikes were parked, but his stomach was spinning like a clothes dryer.

"Well, look who's here," Travis' voice boomed across the pond.

Dylan pretended not to hear. He scrambled down to the water's edge and looked straight out at the boys for the first time. All three were treading water, their arms slung over the log for support. "What do you think you're doing here?" Max yelled.

"Going swimming," Dylan answered as coolly as he could. He unhitched the pack and set it on the ground. There was a loud splash as Jaws dove into the water and began paddling a circle just a few feet from shore.

"Get that mangy mutt out of here," Kevin ordered.

"It's a free country," Dylan said, his voice cracking and finishing high the way he hated.

"Pretty big talk from a nobody like you," Max said.

Dylan bristled. He lunged behind him, grabbed one of Max's checkered sneakers, and flung it up and out. "Go get it, boy," he called to Jaws.

"Why, you little . . ." Max spluttered.

Jaws made a beeline for the sneaker. All three boys started swimming at the same time. Dylan turned and quickly scooped up the bundles of clothes, rifling them as far as he could over the bank.

"Our clothes!" Kevin screamed. Travis tried yelling *thief,* but it sounded more like *thebe* as a mouthful of water choked him off. The boys thrashed even harder toward shore.

"Good dog," Dylan said when Jaws scampered from the water and proudly laid Max's waterlogged sneaker at his feet. Then Dylan took the camera from the pack and pointed it at the incoming trio.

Max was the first to find his footing. "That camera is as much of a goner as you are," he said. But in his haste to climb the pond's steep slope, he lost his balance. When he resurfaced, the other two boys had touched down beside him. Together they surged forward, their faces tight with anger, their eyes locked on Dylan as their bodies grew taller and the water receded.

Dylan waited until the boys were knee-deep.

"Geronimo!" he yelled at the top of his lungs.

"Yeeeeee!" Amy screamed in response, leaping up from her grassy blind as if someone had given her a hot foot. "Bottoms up, you thugs!" Her words split the air, bounced off the surrounding trees, and circled back for an encore. Through the camera's viewer, Dylan watched the boys' faces switch from surprise, to confusion, to horror.

"A GIRL!" Travis shrieked, as if he had seen a body rise from the dead. The boys reeled at the same time. Dylan's finger pressed the shutter button only a fraction of a second before the three shining bodies belly flopped back into the pond. Water sprayed and bubbled around them as their arms and legs slapped frantically, their bodies turning confused circles like whales who had suddenly lost their sonar.

Amy rushed over to Dylan, holding her stomach as the laughter poured out of her. Dylan was on his knees, his eyes teary with his own laughter. Jaws joined in with a steady stream of yelps. Then Max shouted something from the water.

"What's that?" Dylan asked, cupping a hand to his ear.

"She couldn't have seen anything," Max yelled. "It was too quick."

"He's right," Kevin said. "I saw her. She had her hand over her eyes."

"Yeah," Amy said. "Like this." She raised her hand over her eyes, her fingers spread wide apart. "Peek-a-boo," she giggled. "Boy, did I see you!"

"So did the camera," Dylan said. "It's all on film. Now maybe we can solve a few mysteries. Like who wrecked all those papers that day. And who slashed the tires of Mr. B.'s bike."

"You can't prove a thing," Max said defiantly.

"Maybe not," Dylan replied. "But proof won't be necessary once we get a confession."

"Hah!" Max hissed.

"Have it your way," Dylan said. "You might change your mind, though, when you see the next postcard from Gallagher and Robertson, Incorporated. It should be on the racks in a couple of days. I think BOTTOMS UP! would be a good title. And we'll send complimentary copies to every girl in Mrs. Carlson's class."

Max punched his fist into the water, producing a loud thwacking sound.

"Your clothes will be down the road a bit," Dylan said as he reached for Amy's pack. "Just leave a message at the café if you decide to talk."

"And watch you don't get a sunburn," Amy chortled. "I hear it's murder sitting on a scorched behind."

NINETEEN

THE NEXT DAY Amy met Dylan at the café. "I told Gram I was going for a walk," she said. "You should have seen Gramps last night after I told him. He snickered the whole way through dinner. Gram thought he had finally dropped over the edge into senility. But that didn't bother Gramps any. He said if you get something in your head that's funny, you've got to laugh. It's not healthy to hold it in. He said it gives you gas if you do."

As they burst out of the drugstore with the envelope stamped RUSH ORDER, Dylan spotted Travis lurking in the shadows of the realty office across the street. Travis had a newspaper opened in front of him. He kept lowering the paper and peeking over the top.

"Do you see what I see?" Dylan asked.

"Poor Travis," Amy answered. "He'll never make a spy."

"Max must have sent him to tail us," Dylan said. "Probably wants to know if we're really going through with this."

Dylan hadn't given much thought to what he would do if the picture didn't come out. But now, as he sat down on the curb, he realized Max had given him a golden opportunity. With Travis looking on, Dylan need only pretend the snapshot came out. Even if it were all blurry or overexposed, Travis would never know.

"Ready?" Dylan asked, ripping open the envelope. Amy crossed her fingers. "I guess," she said.

Dylan prepared himself to laugh or to cry out for Travis's sake. But the whistle that shot through his lips when the picture appeared wasn't fake in the least. Nor was the shriek that burst from Amy before she dropped her face in her hands, her shoulders shaking uncontrollably.

"Wow," Dylan said. "Wow!" He held up the photo to study it further. Another whistle escaped his lips. He glanced over at Travis who quickly ducked behind his paper like a rabbit disappearing down its hole at the sight of danger. Except that Travis wasn't really hidden at all. His chubby legs and arms remained as visible as ever. Dylan smiled. Travis needed a bigger hole.

Amy lifted her head. Her face was tinged with red. She took the photo from Dylan and inspected it closely. "The girls back home will never believe this," she said. "I can *barely* believe it myself."

Dylan laughed. Looking again at the picture, he saw victory. "You know," he said. "The photograph *is* mightier than the sword."

*

152

The blue flag popped in the breeze. Dylan halted at the entrance to the fort. He started to give the password, then realized that it no longer mattered. Max, Kevin, and Travis sat cross-legged around the ring of colored rocks in the middle. Dylan stepped inside, and the boys jumped up.

"That girl isn't with you, is she?" Kevin asked, craning his head to see through the doorway.

"Her name is Amy," Dylan answered. "No, it's just me, like we planned."

Travis jabbed a hand into the bag of corn chips he was holding. He chucked a load of chips into his mouth. "How do we know this isn't another trick?" he said.

Dylan made an X over his heart with his thumb to show that his word was good. He looked at Max.

Max was tossing and catching a stone with one hand. He kept shifting his weight from one foot to the other as if he had to go to the bathroom. "You got the picture?" he asked.

Dylan nodded and reached for his back pocket. "Of course the negative is locked away for safekeeping," he said. "I'm sure you can understand why." He held out the snapshot. The boys rushed forward, and Max yanked the photo out of Dylan's hand.

"Holy moly!" Kevin gasped. "We're done for."

Travis's jaw dropped, revealing a mouthful of half-chewed chips. "Dylan, you can't do this to us," he sputtered.

"It could be worse," Dylan said matter-of-factly. "Lucky you turned around in time. But even from the back it's a real beauty, don't you think? No trouble telling who's who. The color adds a nice touch." He gazed at Max's shock of bright orange hair, forcing himself to hold back a smile.

"This is blackmail!" Max thundered, whipping the stone against the side of the fort.

"Call it what you like," Dylan replied. "Fact is, if you three don't admit to slashing the tires and pay up, this picture will be on every postcard rack in Seaview."

"No one would ever put it up," Kevin countered. "It's . . . it's dirty."

"There's nothing dirty about the human body," Dylan said. "And Mrs. Allioto thinks the picture is cute."

"You showed it to *her*?" Travis cried.

Dylan shrugged. "Why not? Amy said we needed to check out our markets first. Amy's a professional, you know."

Travis rammed the bottom of his palm against his forehead. "We're cooked," he moaned.

Kevin turned to Max. "We gotta do what he says. We'll be the laughingstocks of the whole town."

"Shut up and let me think," Max muttered. For a second, Dylan almost felt sorry for Max as he watched him searching for a way out. But there was no way out. Max would simply have to own up.

"How do we know you won't go ahead and publish this even if we do confess?" Max said finally.

"I give you my word that I won't," Dylan said.

Max snorted as if that would never do.

Dylan felt his jaw tighten. "It will have to be enough for you," he said. "The word of a nobody. The word of a convict's son." He swallowed hard and looked straight into Max's eyes. He could feel the anger bubbling up inside him. But the anger was only partly directed at Max. The other half was directed at himself for believing all that stuff about his being a nobody, about his having bad blood because of his father.

"I'm no cheat, and I don't lie," he continued, his voice rising. "I may be stuck with my father, but I'm no thief either. I'm me . . . Dylan Robertson. One of a kind. And my word is as good as anyone's."

TWENTY

DYLAN LEAPT FOR the phone. It was Mr. Bronski. Max and his father had just left the shop.

"I think young Max will be grounded for a while," Mr. Bronski said. "His dad was about to blow a gasket. The other two boys called and said they were sorry and that they would bring in the money tomorrow. They all must have had a change of heart."

Dylan decided to save the story for later. He wanted to see Mr. B.'s face when he told him about the photo. "Amy and I sort of made them an offer they couldn't refuse," he said.

Mr. Bronski cleared his throat. "Yeah, well, that's not all I called for. I thought you'd want to know that I finally sold that old orange Honda."

Wham! Dylan felt as though the wind had been knocked out of him. He took a deep breath and pressed his eyes closed with his fingers. Well, it was stupid to think the bike would be there forever, he told himself. Anybody with an ounce of brains would know better than to bet on something so chancy.

"Dylan? Are you still there?"

"Yeah, I was just thinking is all. Thanks for calling, Mr. B."

"Wait! Don't you want to know who I sold it to?"

"It doesn't matter."

"It should. I sold the bike to you. That is, if you're still interested."

"Me?" Dylan shouted. "What do you mean?"

"Just what I said. I'm putting your eighty dollars toward the purchase price of the bike. I figure you're good for the other seventy and thought why not sell it to you now. You can pay in installments, however much you can afford a month, until it's paid off."

"But . . ."

"Oh," Mr. Bronski said, sounding disappointed. "Not interested, huh? Well, it was a crazy idea of mine. I get them all the time. You can ask my wife. No, on second thought, don't ask her. She's still steaming over my idea to plant pumpkins between the rows of corn. Those bleeping pumpkins nearly choked out the whole corn crop this year."

"Mr. B., that's great!"

"Great for the pumpkins, not too hot for the corn."

"No," Dylan cried. "I mean about the bike. Of course I want to buy it. I just can't believe it. I mean, it's something I've wanted for so long, it doesn't seem possible it's happening."

"Well, if it will make it seem any more real to you, you can stop by soon and look at the SOLD sign that's sitting on the bike. And when you come down we can talk about how to get that old machine prettied up. Okay?"

Okay? Dylan thought. *Okay?* It was much better than that. The word that came to mind was the one Mrs. Allioto had used in the café the day she found out she was a grandmother. She was nearly bursting with pride and happiness.

Yes, that's the way he felt now. Much better than super or wonderful or terrific.

"Fan-*tas*-ti-co!" he yelled into the phone.

*

Dylan tried calling Amy four times that night to tell her the good news. Twice the line was busy, and twice Mrs. Gallagher answered.

Amy was waiting for him on the front porch when Dylan rode up with the paper early the next morning.

"I called you last night," he said, hopping off his bike.

"You twit," Amy said. "So it was you. Why'd you hang up?"

"You know why. Your grandmother made it pretty clear she doesn't like me."

She made a face. "I think Gram has gotten over all that. Gramps and I told her about the pond and the photo. She admitted the idea was a good one considering the circumstances. I think she's sorry for the way she treated you. She said sometimes a person just can't see things straight no matter how old they are."

Amy raised her fist in a victory salute when Dylan told her about Mr. Bronski's phone call. "I'd do my Indian celebration dance," she said. "But I'm afraid I'm not quite up to it today." She pulled in her lips and looked away.

"But we did it," Dylan said. "We won! Aren't you happy?"

"Of course I'm happy. I mean, I'm happy about that. It's just that I'll miss this place. That's all."

"What are you talking about? You've still got a week left."

She shook her head. "We got a cable last night. Mom and Dad are coming home early. Dad's been sick. The doctor in Europe said it'd be best if he cut the trip short and came home to rest." She paused, her shoulders sagging. "I'm kind of worried about Dad. Mom wouldn't let on no matter how bad it was. Not in a cable from way over there."

Dylan slumped like a marionette whose strings have been suddenly cut.

"I'm hoping for the best," Amy added. "All I know is that Dad will want me to be there when he gets back, no matter what. String Bean is meeting me at the airport."

"When?" Dylan asked.

"I should get into Chicago at about eight tonight. Gram's helping me pack right now. I told her I'd like to walk on the beach one more time. You'll come, won't you?"

Dylan nodded. "I'm sorry about your father," he said.

*

They walked barefoot, letting the wet sand ooze between their toes.

"Do you think you'll be moving?" Amy asked.

"Hard to tell. Depends on Mom. I thought I really wanted to at first, but I'm not so sure now."

"Well, one thing for sure, you won't have to worry about those bullies anymore. Those fellows bit off more than they could swallow when they tangled with the likes of us."

"I wasn't thinking about them," Dylan said. "I mean, I like Aunt Jolene a whole lot and all, but moving to the desert doesn't seem quite right." He looked out past the surf to where a ship was making its way like a toy boat across the horizon. "I don't know. It just feels like home here. I don't think we've ever been in one place this long before."

"I know what you mean," Amy said. "As much as I badmouth Chicago, it'd be tough leaving it. I guess a place really grows on you after a while."

They watched a flock of gulls turn in midflight, the birds' underbellies and wings flashing silver as they caught the sun.

"What about your dad?" Amy said when the birds had soared from view. "I know it's none of my business, but you've hardly mentioned him since I've been here."

"What's to mention?" Dylan said. "I told you, he's locked up."

"He'll be getting out, won't he?"

"Yes."

"What then?"

Dylan shrugged. It wasn't much of an answer. But it was true. He didn't know what would happen. Nor did he understand how you could hate someone and miss them at the same time. The two weren't supposed to go together.

"It took me months to forgive my real dad once I was old enough to realize he wasn't coming back," Amy said.

"Well, he shouldn't have run off like that."

"No. But he did. That's the point. So I gave him the *what for* in my mind, and I felt a lot better."

"I felt pretty good giving Max and the guys the *what for* at the fort the other day," Dylan said.

"Same kind of thing," she replied.

When they got back to Amy's, Dylan said, "I'll be sure to send you half of whatever else comes in on the cards." He wanted to ask if she might be coming back to Seaview next summer. Maybe they could come up with a new card. Keep the business going. But he thought it was pretty crazy to be thinking about that already. Instead, he said, "I should write down my address in case you ever feel like writing or something."

Amy ran inside and returned with a pencil and pad. She had a paper bag tucked under her arm. After they had exchanged addresses, Amy handed Dylan the bag. "For you," she said. "It should fit." Folded up inside was the black T-shirt her mother had sent from London. Dylan held up the shirt and read the words to himself: THE PHOTOGRAPH IS MIGHTIER THAN THE SWORD.

"Thanks," he said.

"*De nada*," Amy replied. "That's Spanish for *it's nothing*. I learned it from String Bean. He took a course last year."

"I guess I'd better go," Dylan said when Mrs. Gallagher called for Amy a moment later. He reached in his pocket and took out the sand dollar. "Here," he said. "Keep it. Still not a chip in it. It'll be triple lucky in Chicago since there aren't any sand dollars there."

Amy smiled her thanks.

Just then, Jaws nosed open the door and bounded out. Dylan dropped to his knees to meet the dog's playful charge.

"He's already looking forward to his ice cream reward when we get back," Amy said. "Say *chocolate*, boy."

"*Roof!*" Jaws answered.

Amy giggled. "Still the smartest dog on either side of the Mississippi."

"You don't have to tell me," Dylan said.

Mrs. Gallagher stepped onto the porch. "Amy, we've got tons to do yet."

Dylan raised his hand in a shy wave.

"Hello, Dylan," Mrs. Gallagher said. "Mr. Gallagher said to tell you to feel free to stop by and chat anytime you want. I'd like it if you did too."

Dylan nodded. He gave Jaws a final pat, then grabbed his bike, feeling a lump in his throat when he looked at Amy. "See you," he said.

"Take care," she replied. "Happy biking. And tell Mr. B. bye for me."

He rode out the drive. The lump in his throat stayed with him all the way to the café.

TWENTY-ONE

"SPADES," DYLAN SAID, slapping down an eight.

His mother frowned. "Thanks a lot. Where'd you get all those eights?"

She picked up two new cards from the deck and reluctantly added them to the others she was holding. They were playing Crazy Eights on the steps of the cottage. The lamp from inside offered just enough light through the open door.

"Mr. Gallagher says Amy's dad is going to be all right," Dylan said as he rid his hand of a dreaded fifteen-point ace. "I guess he tried to see too much in Europe. But he's okay now."

His mother's face brightened. "I'm glad to hear that. Really glad. I suppose it must have been hard on Amy not knowing how things stood when she left."

"Amy's pretty brave," Dylan replied. "She said her father would need her no matter what."

As the game went on, Dylan found it harder and harder to concentrate. He debated a long time over which card to throw before picking out the queen and plunking it on his mother's seven.

"Wrong card, bucko," his mother cried as she matched his queen. "Thank you kindly. It's about time I won a hand."

He laid down his two remaining cards.

"Looks like you got caught napping," she teased when she saw the two face cards.

He hadn't been napping. Just thinking. He started to say as much but had to stop to clear the frog from his throat.

"Mom."

"Hmm?"

"I was wondering. How's Dad doing?—I mean, you said he was sick that time."

"That was just a cold," she said as she tallied the score. "Passed in about a week."

"Does he . . . does he ever talk about me?"

She swung her head up, her eyes round with surprise. "Are you kidding? You're the first *and* the last thing he talks about. He's even written you letters, but he never sends them. I've offered to deliver the letters, but he says it wouldn't be any good that way." She paused. "Haven't I told you all this before?"

"I guess I forgot."

He watched her shuffle the cards. The tiny earrings in her ears shone like gold-colored teardrops as she leaned over and dealt. The earrings were a gift from his father. They weren't real gold, Dylan knew. But they looked nice, and his mother had always treated them as if they were worth a lot of money.

"Are you going to stay with Dad when he gets out?"

It was a question he had been wanting to ask for a long time, but he had never been able to drum up the courage. He figured it was because he had always been afraid of the answer. He'd been afraid of a lot of things lately.

She clasped her arms around her knees, as if to steady herself. "Yes," she said firmly. "Marriages aren't easy to save these days, no matter what the situation. But I'm willing to give it one more shot."

Her eyes narrowed. "Of course things will be different. I've already made that clear to your father. We're going to find a place and stay put. Maybe in Seaview, maybe not. But once we decide, that's it. No more moving around."

She looked straight at Dylan. "I've been doing some thinking. Seems to me people are a lot like plants. You keep uprooting them, they eventually die. Every transplant is a trauma. We've had our share of traumas."

"But Dad's a crook," Dylan said. "He'll always be a crook."

She sighed. "I don't believe in 'always' anything," she said. "I know he made a mistake. He's made a few in his time. But he's more than his mistakes. Much more. If I didn't believe that, I'd have packed up long ago. You and I would be long gone."

Dylan slid his bare foot over the pebbled concrete of the step. In a few months his father would be out on parole. He got the jitters just thinking about it. It was like being in one of those haunted houses people set up for Halloween. He didn't look forward to having his father jump out at him like some clanky old skeleton.

"Well," he said finally. "One thing for sure, I'd like to tell Dad a few things."

"I think you should," she replied.

"He won't like what I've got to say."

"Some things have to be said," she answered, her hand falling over his and pressing lightly.

*

There were no dark closet-rooms. No screens. The room was large. One whole wall was covered with tall windows. The bars made tic-tac-toe patterns behind the glass.

Dylan followed his mother to one of the tables off to the left. His mother laid her purse and the box of cookies on the table. "It's not usually a long wait." she said. "You okay?"

He sat without answering, focusing on one of the nearby tables. A little boy was playing with a toy train beside the table. A woman sat at the table, opposite a man in blue. The two were holding hands and talking quietly. The boy made loud *choo-choo* sounds as he pushed the train between the legs of the man's chair.

Dylan's mother looked across the room. She waved. "There's Betty. We've gotten to be friends. I promised her a recipe—it'll only take a second. Want to meet her?"

He shook his head.

"Be right back." she said.

He followed her stride across the room, then turned to eye the big double doors where two guards stood watch. More than anything, he wished Amy could be here. Amy would say something funny. Help him get rid of the knot that was twisting in the pit of his stomach. He put a hand there where it hurt, against the fabric of the shirt. Amy's shirt.

The boy with the train had crawled onto the man's lap. The man wrapped his hands around the boy and started moving his leg up and down, giving the boy a ride. The boy laughed.

You're a sea monster, Dad! Give me a ride.

There was a loud crash of metal on metal behind the big double doors. The doors slid open. Dylan leapt up at the sight of his father. He turned to find his mother. She was still talking; way over there. How could she?

The blue uniform stopped in front of the table. Dylan read the numbers over the pocket. There was a seven somewhere in the middle. His father's lips were pinched closed. The ends of the mustache spread outward with the start of a smile.

"You've grown. Hasn't been that long. But you've grown."

It was the same voice.

Dylan stuck his hands in his pockets, then lifted them out again. He looked beyond his father's shoulder to the clock on the wall, his eyes following the sweep of the second hand.

"Might as well sit down, don't you think?"

The knot pushed against the walls of Dylan's stomach as he sat. He watched his father lift the lid of the cookie box. They were molasses. The box slid toward him.

"Have one?"

"I didn't come here to eat cookies."

The man nodded. His hair was cut shorter than usual. Not quite as short as Tod Lindholst's. But short.

"I'm glad you came. You have no idea how good it is to see you. I've been wanting to—"

"No," Dylan said, his fists clenching. "Don't. I've got something to say first."

He felt his eyes start to burn. He could hear his breath pumping in and out . . . "Like you'd better not hurt Mom again! And no more promises unless you mean to keep them."

The man's eyes moved as if he was going to speak. Dylan held up his hand, whipping his head back and forth once in a forceful NO.

"I bought the bike with my own money," he almost shouted. "All on my own. I wasn't going to wait for you. I wouldn't want your kind of money anyway. And the bike . . . it's starting to look like new. It's really something. Mr. Bronski's been helping me. But it's much too small for you, so don't get any ideas about riding it. You'll have to get your own if you want one." The words kept pouring out. "And if you . . . if you mess up again—Mom and me, we'll take off. Make our own roots. Just like that. Got it? You got it, Dad?"

Dylan's heart was beating like mad. He turned his head away, because tears were filling his eyes. He hadn't planned on the tears. "Heck with it," he said, sniffling up the wet from his nose. "Just to heck with it."

The faces and heads of the people on the other side of the room swam in the blur. When Dylan looked back, his father's eyes had become dark lakes. There were teeth marks on the man's bottom lip.

Dylan rubbed a fist across his cheek to clear the tears. He saw his father's arm move forward. Slowly. So slowly, it hardly seemed to be moving at all. But it *was* moving. Reaching across the table toward him. And Dylan thought of the starfish he and Amy had seen on the beach. Growing a new arm. Could they really? Was it possible?

He let his own hand inch forward. Felt the warmth of his father's palm, the pressure as their fingers locked together. His chest filled with air. His eyelids pressed closed.

Dylan didn't know how many seconds passed before he felt his father's grip loosen. He opened his eyes and pulled back his hand—his fingers curling into his palms as though protecting something small and precious that he had found on the beach.

"That's what I get for going with molasses," his mother said, rushing up to the table. "Two of the world's all-time biggest cookie lovers, and not a bite between them. I can take a hint."

Her smile broke for an instant, her lips quivering as she looked from Dylan to her husband. The man rose. Dylan watched his parents embrace. When the two had sat down, Dylan noticed the puzzled look on his father's face.

"Never seen a shirt like that before."

Dylan sat up straighter so all the letters could be seen. "It's a gift from a friend," he said. "Someone you don't know. There's a real story behind it."

"Care to share? Nothing like a good story."

"It's a long one," Dylan answererd. "I wouldn't know where to begin. Besides, I might not have time to finish it."

"You could start," his father said. The voice thinned suddenly. "There's always next week."

"I'd love to hear the whole thing myself," his mother put in eagerly. "I've a feeling I was only told what was absolutely necessary at the time. We poor mothers are always left in the dark."

Dylan blew out a sigh. Maybe it wasn't such a bad idea. At least it would pass the time. He rubbed his hands on his pants as he gathered his thoughts.

"It started at the café . . . that's where I work, Dad . . . maybe you didn't know . . . Mrs. Allioto's . . . I needed the job because of the bike . . . and this strange girl tapped me on the shoulder and asked if I had any bones."

"Bones?"

"Bones," Dylan said. "For Jaws . . . like the famous shark, only this Jaws eats bubble-gum ice cream instead of people, and—"

"Slow down," his father said. "You're going too fast. This story sounds like a winner. I want to savor it."

Dylan looked at his mother, who winked back, her face beaming.

"Okay," he said. "Let's see . . . where was I?"

"Something about a famous shark who eats bubble-gum ice cream," his father said.

"Not a *shark*! A *dog*!" Dylan said with a laugh. He shook his head. At this rate, he'd be lucky to get even halfway through the story before next week.

9 780595 153268